THE VIOLET DAWN

HUMANITY SERIES - BOOK THREE

SETH RAIN

Copyright © 2020 by Seth Rain

All rights reserved.

No part of this book may be reproduced in any form or by any electronic or mechanical means, including information storage and retrieval systems, without written permission from the author, except for the use of brief quotations in a book review.

Published by Human Fiction

ISBN 978-1-9162775-2-6

Copy Editing: Jane Hammett

Proofreading: Johanna Robinson

Cover Design: Damonza

YOUR FREE NOVELLA IS WAITING!

Visit **sethrain.com** to download your free digital copy of the prequel novella: *The Rogue Watcher* and sign up to Seth's Reading Group emails.

A BRIEF NOTE

I have used British English spelling throughout this series of books. Not only am I a Brit, but this story is set in Britain, and so it seems only right to use British English spelling. I hope this does not detract from your enjoyment.

Seth.

For Callum

"Only when humanity developed the tools and the ideas to observe and analyse the bewildering spectacle of the clear night sky did the cosmos begin to awaken from its ignorance."

Taken from *Novacene* (2019) by James Lovelock

THE VIOLET DAWN

ONE

SCOTT HAD CONSIDERED GIVING up many times. No matter what he did, no matter where he went, eventually they always found him.

He hid his arms behind his back. It had been eighteen years since George, with the help of a surgical-machine, had removed his left hand.

The young Watcher's revolver rattled in his fist. 'Which one of you is Scott?'

George, next to Scott, also on his knees, didn't flinch.

'Show me your hands,' the Watcher said. His face flushed, revealing faint whiskers scattered across his chin. He couldn't be any older than twenty.

'What I don't understand,' George said, 'is why you don't want to go to Heaven yourself.'

'Which one of you is Scott?'

'I'm Scott,' George said.

The Watcher's eyes shifted from one to the other. Scott lifted his arms slowly and showed his missing hand.

The Watcher shifted his weight, his expression pained. His grip tightened around the handle of the revolver. 'My time will come. As it will for those in hiding.' He cleared his throat. 'What do you know about those in Liverpool?'

Scott noticed George hold his breath. Neither of them knew anything about survivors in Liverpool.

'Why would we tell you?' Scott asked.

The Watcher raised an eyebrow at Scott. 'I have to kill you.' He turned to George. 'But if *you* want to offer some information, then we might be able to come to some agreement. We know of several gatherings across the UK. There is one group living in Liverpool. It will be better for them if we find them sooner rather than later.'

'Okay,' George said.

Scott snapped his head around to stare at George. The Watcher appeared surprised, too.

'I'll tell you,' George said. 'A group from Liverpool? Well, what I do know is that their best album was *Revolver*.'

The Watcher was clearly confused.

Scott shook his head. 'If you're going to antagonise him, can you do it with references he will understand?'

The Watcher's face darkened. 'Mathew wants me to pass on a message before your time comes to meet God Almighty.'

Scott waited.

The young Watcher's lips flickered silently, as though recalling the line.

'Let me guess,' George said. 'I miss you.'

'Stop!' the Watcher said.

Scott glanced across at George. He was trying to buy time, but aggravating the Watcher would only make him nervous – and perhaps act hastily.

The Watcher stared into Scott's eyes. 'Mathew wants me to tell you: he will find her and tell her the truth.'

George glanced at Scott, then back at the Watcher.

'That's it?' George asked. 'That's all he has to say? He's not been able to catch us in eighteen years and that's all he has to say?' He turned to Scott. 'Tell who the truth?'

'I've no idea,' Scott said.

The Watcher appeared surprised.

'How old are you?' Scott asked him.

The Watcher shook his head and frowned. 'What does that have to do with anything? I'm here to send you to Him.'

'And yet, here we are, still alive,' George said.

The young Watcher grimaced.

'You've given us the message,' George said, 'now do we get the line?' He cleared his throat. 'The whole "this empty chamber belongs to Him" spiel.'

The Watcher took a step backwards.

'You've not said it before, have you?' George asked. 'This is your first time.'

The Watcher's head turned left and right, the revolver shaking even more.

'Can you believe it?' George said, turning to Scott. 'Mathew's getting desperate.'

'Stop!' the Watcher said. 'Stop. I'm sending you both to Him. What I'm doing is a good thing. It is a mercy.'

Scott sighed. He considered telling the Watcher that they'd brainwashed him, how what he was saying was nonsense, grounded in nothing but a fairy tale. But, looking into the young man's eyes, he saw there was no point.

'You're scared,' Scott said. 'If you were sure this was the right thing to do, you wouldn't be scared. And you wouldn't have that look in your eyes.'

He felt George's eyes on him too.

The Watcher blinked quickly.

'What you're doing is murder,' Scott said. 'Mathew will

tell you otherwise. But the truth is: you're about to murder two innocent people.'

The Watcher's eyes opened wide, as though remembering something important. 'But you're not innocent. None of us are innocent. We're all sinners. Every one of us. And this is the price we must pay.'

'Great,' George muttered.

'I am freeing you from this sin,' the Watcher said. 'I'm freeing your souls so they can return to Him.'

'I'm bored,' George said. 'Are we going to do this or what?'

For a moment, the Watcher appeared hurt. He rubbed the back of his head with his free hand and took two deep breaths, then pointed the revolver at Scott.

'The Watcher's revolver has five bullets and one empty chamber. This emp—'

'Hang on,' George said.

The Watcher's face turned even redder.

'Have you turned the chamber thing? The cylinder?' George mimed the action.

'Be quiet,' the Watcher snapped.

'It's just,' George went on, 'if this really is His doing, then don't you have to make sure there's a one-in-six chance we survive?'

The Watcher exhaled loudly through his nose. 'Stop talking,' he said.

George relaxed his arms. 'It's just, seeing as you've not done this before, I don't want you to make a mistake. Imagine shooting us and then afterwards, realising you didn't spin the chamber thing.'

The Watcher glanced at the gun, then wiped his brow with the back of his other hand.

'Point that thing at me!' George growled, his tone changing. 'At me!'

'No,' Scott said.

The Watcher's hand shook violently.

'Shoot me,' George said.

The Watcher spoke quickly: 'The Watcher's revolver has five bullets and one empty chamber. This empty chamber belongs to Him, to do with as He wishes.'

Scott glanced at George, who closed his eyes.

'No,' Scott said to the Watcher. 'Don't do this!'

The revolver in the young Watcher's hand trembled.

'Don't!' Scott said. 'Mathew will never know. Turn around and leave.'

The Watcher's bottom lip trembled, and tears welled in his eyes.

'Wait,' Scott said.

The revolver went off. Scott fell back, raising both arms to shield his face. George, out of the corner of his eye, jolted backwards, his head crashing against the wall behind. Blood covered the floor next to Scott. The Watcher held the revolver in both hands, staring at it.

Scott couldn't hear anything except a dull, high-pitched whistle. He hadn't thought the Watcher would do it. Now, the revolver smoking, the man's eyes wide open, he appeared even younger than he had before.

Scott stared at the Watcher, then at George's body, then back at the Watcher who lowered the revolver and shook his head.

'What have you done?' Scott asked.

The Watcher stared at George's body. 'He is with Him.' Slowly, he nodded.

'No,' Scott said. 'He is dead. And you killed him.'

The Watcher's face was pale. He wrapped an arm around his stomach and turned away to throw up.

Scott leapt up, running into the Watcher and knocking him over. His revolver skidded across the floor. The difference in age was there immediately; he was young, agile, much quicker. The Watcher turned Scott around and wrapped an arm around his neck. Scott thrust his head backwards and felt the Watcher's nose break against the back of his skull. The Watcher cried out in pain and fell backwards. Scott dived for the revolver and turned it on the young man, who tried to get to his feet but slipped. Breathing deeply, his throat sore, his muscles spasming, Scott's head still buzzed from the revolver going off.

The young Watcher cowered against the wall, his hands raised. Even after everything he'd said about God, about doing the right thing, death scared him. Scott lowered the gun. As he did so he heard movement in the hall. Eve and Elidi ran in, Eve's gun pointed at the Watcher on the ground.

Eve looked over at George, dead on the floor. 'What did you do?' she shouted at the Watcher.

The Watcher's eyes opened wide and he gasped. 'It's you!' he said, his eyes fixed on Eve. 'It's you.'

'Wait,' Scott said, reaching out to stop her.

But her gun fired once, twice, then a third time.

The young Watcher was still, blood pooling around him.

Scott couldn't move. He could only watch as Eve and Elidi bent over George, trying to stop the bleeding.

Finally Eve stood up and turned to him, her violet eyes sombre.

TWO

SCOTT OPENED his eyes to see Eve sitting on the bed.

'I'm sorry George didn't make it,' she said.

Scott nodded. George had been his best friend since the day he met him walking along the motorway. He died an old man and this gave Scott some consolation, but only a little. There would be a time for him to mourn George properly. For now, all they could do was perform the ritual: burn the body.

'You tried,' he said. 'You did everything you could.'

'How did it happen?' she asked. 'How did we get caught out like that?'

'Mathew is finding more and more young men willing to become Watchers. He couldn't have been any older than you. He can't have been much older than eighteen.'

She lowered her head and stared at the bed sheets. 'I normally know when they're close by. Why didn't I know?'

'You've kept us safe from Watchers many times before. Don't blame yourself.'

'I should have known.'

For so long, Eve had honed her ability to detect danger.

It wasn't obvious how she did it, but Scott often thought it had something to do with what Mathew had told him. All her senses, heightened maybe by the AI's manipulation of her genetics, came together in a way that made her hyper-alert to the approach of people she didn't know. He couldn't be sure, but sometimes he noticed Eve sniffing the air or narrowing her eyes before warning him.

'I shot him,' she said. 'The Watcher. I didn't stop to think. I just shot.'

Scott wanted to tell her she'd done the right thing. But there was something in the Watcher's eyes, in the way he'd retreated from what he'd done, as though he didn't understand.

'I didn't think,' she said. 'Sometimes it feels like it's not me. You know?'

Scott paused. He could see a pleading in Eve's eyes. She wanted him to agree with her.

'You know?' she asked again.

'Of course,' he said. 'At times like that, it's difficult to think. You saw he'd hurt George, and you reacted. It's only natural.'

Eve nodded slowly, biting her bottom lip. 'Why would they want to do that?'

'Watchers?' Scott winced in pain, reaching around to his back as he shifted on the bed. 'It gives them purpose. I think it gives them a reason for why things are the way they are. More now than ever.'

'But now's the time to rebel against Mathew. What he's done is wrong. Why don't they see it? It's obvious.'

'We need to leave,' Scott said. There was no time to discuss it. 'Mathew will know we're here.'

Eve stood. 'I've already told everyone.'

Scott nodded, knowing full well Eve would already have

set in motion what needed to be done. She was clever – always had been. It was her idea to use the bigger cities. Manchester was big, and at first there were plenty of places in which to disappear. Hiding in cities had worked for a long time.

Scott followed Eve out of the hotel and stood between two towering buildings. They were the tallest in the UK; the second, only a few hundred metres from the first, was built by a competing company. The extra two floors were a way of claiming superiority, not only in height, but in computing power. The first tower was the headquarters of Soteria, the maker of nearly all self-drivers. Scott turned to the taller of the two towers. Above the entrance was a sign: *MYND*. Their creations were the closest thing to believable-looking human robotics. They'd made billions selling 'companions'.

'Where to?' Eve asked.

Scott turned back to the hotel, waiting for the rest of them.

'I'm thinking north,' Scott said.

'Back to the Lakes?' she asked, frowning. 'They'll be waiting for us.'

Scott stroked his chin.

'I know you miss them,' she said. 'But enough to risk it?'

Scott considered it. If he was alone and didn't have Eve and the others to think about, maybe he'd go back. He saw the rest of them come out of the hotel doors. He shook his head. 'No.'

'I'm thinking Wales,' she said. 'Mathew won't suspect that. There'd be no reason to. What about the people in Liverpool? The survivors the Watcher told you about?'

'That was a trap,' Scott said.

Eve waited, her eyes narrowing. 'I don't think it is. He was going to kill you – there was no reason for him to lie.'

Eve often said things that Scott thought were far too old, too knowing for someone of eighteen.

The hotel entrance and the pavement outside were covered in weeds. Plants emerged through every crack, clinging to the walls of the hotel. The earth was reaching up to reclaim the city.

Elidi was the first out of the building, leading the way.

'Have you counted?' Scott asked her.

'Sixteen,' she said.

Scott peered around her to look at the women and children. He recalled the last time he'd asked, when George had still been alive, and the response was seventeen.

Elidi had a son, Daker, who was always close by, unless she and Eve were out on patrol. Then Daker stayed close to Gavin. Elidi's husband, Faisal, had been killed by two men in Glasgow three years earlier. They had kidnapped two of the women and left Faisal for dead. Scott found him lying in the street, his chest cut open – a message to anyone else thinking of going back there.

Scott checked his bag for the box the AI had told him to take, all those years ago. He'd considered destroying it hundreds of times. But something had stopped him each time; maybe it was the connection to Eve, or that it was too special to destroy so readily.

Eve led the way to where they'd hidden the bus, in a tunnel, half a mile from the hotel. Scott waited for everyone to board, counting as he watched them. There was only one other man left, and he was barely a man: Gavin. He was the last on the bus, checking behind, then nodding to Scott. He hovered near Eve, apparently waiting for something. Eve didn't acknowledge him, so Gavin strode away towards the back of the bus.

'You could throw him a bone now and then,' Scott said, getting onto the bus.

Without looking at Scott, Eve adjusted the driver's seat. 'I don't want to encourage him. Wouldn't be right.'

Scott saw that Gavin was in a seat near the rear, his head resting against the window.

'Guess you're right,' Scott said. 'But still.'

Eve's expression told him to give it up.

He held up his hand in surrender. 'Okay, okay. It's just—'

'Just nothing,' she said, starting the engine. 'It's not like he has a lot of females to choose from. I'm the only woman he knows who's even close to his own age. He's a teenage boy – of course he's interested.'

'I don't think it's just that,' Scott said. 'I think he really likes you.'

Eve's face softened.

'Just talk to him,' Scott said. 'Tell him you're not interested in him like that – but you'd like to stay friends.'

Eve gripped the steering wheel. 'I will,' she said. 'Now will you leave it, Dad?'

'Thank you,' Scott said. 'Are you going to get us out of here or what?'

Eve opened her eyes wide, ready to reprimand him.

Scott smiled, and Eve shook her head.

At times like this, he doubted what Mathew had told him. It was in Mathew's interest to make Scott believe Eve was half AI. Scott didn't know what to think. He didn't want to believe it. But it was always there. Her eyes troubled him. When the light was right, her eyes were a shade of violet he'd never seen before. Most of the time, her eyes were brown, but now and then they shifted and Scott was sure he saw, in the violet swirl of her irises, tiny ones and zeros – like when she'd entered the room and shot the Watcher.

In moments of stress, of heightened emotions, something changed in her. He'd never spoken to her about what Mathew had told him. He'd not spoken to anyone about it. At times, he'd considered telling George, but he'd never plucked up the courage to go through with it; it would have been a betrayal. But there were moments, like when he saw the shift of violet in her eyes, that he held his breath and felt a tightening in his chest. He knew something so fundamental about her, which she did not know. He'd let everyone, including Eve, assume he was her father. It was easier that way. He'd told her as much as he could about her mother, but had to invent much of her history, and lie about her age to coincide with his own.

Eve drove the bus out of the city.

Gavin, used to recovering from Eve's rejections, was on lookout, surveying the streets behind to ensure they weren't being followed. Scott played along now and then, giving Gavin a thumbs-up, asking if everything was as it should be. Gavin gave Scott a serious look and nodded, or returned his thumbs-up.

'So where to?' Eve asked again.

Scott pointed at the window to the motorway.

'Wales,' he said. 'There's no reason for Mathew to suspect that.'

'Good idea,' Eve said, pushing her foot down on the accelerator. 'Wish I'd thought of that.'

Scott gripped her shoulder and squeezed.

'What about north Wales?' she asked. 'I know you like mountains.'

Scott nodded. 'Sounds good to me.'

'What about the survivors in Liverpool?' she asked.

Scott checked on the women, children and Gavin; they'd all become dependent on him and on Eve. He'd played it safe, and it had worked. Many had died or had left, but most of them had stayed together.

'No,' he said. 'We can't risk it. We should bide our time.'

Eve didn't answer. Instead, she kept her eyes on the road ahead.

THREE

SCOTT SAT on the front seat of the coach behind Eve. Now George was gone, he felt even more responsible for those on the bus, although Eve was making more of the important decisions; it was Eve the children spoke to, looking for reassurance. And there was Elidi, the nominated spokesperson for the group. The women had always been mistrustful of Scott – maybe, he thought, because he was male. Once, Elidi had explained to Scott why the group consisted mainly of women and children. Scott couldn't remember what her reasoning was, exactly. But, in the eighteen years he'd been on the run with the rest of them, their numbers had risen to fifty-two, but had then dropped to sixteen. Nearly all of those who had died were men: old men, middle-aged men, young men – there didn't seem to be any consistency or pattern. They joined the group then left the group just as quickly, almost as though they had an innate desire to find trouble, to search it out. Now there was only Gavin. Scott wanted to help him survive and to try help him think clearly, to stay close to the group, to avoid doing anything foolish. He'd thought maybe Gavin would be the one he could trust with everything he knew and had kept to himself. The women wouldn't let him get too close to them, but Gavin was friendly and respected him.

After a couple of hours, Eve pulled off the road and down a farm track, heading for a barn Scott had spotted from the motorway. They needed more diesel, and Scott had become accustomed to spotting the best places to find it.

The women and children filled the tank and the empty cans with diesel.

'What did the Watcher mean?' Eve asked, surprising Scott. He turned to see her behind him.

'What?'

'I've been thinking about it. The Watcher. He said: "It's you."'

Scott knew what the Watcher had meant, but he wasn't ready to share that with Eve. 'I don't know. I don't think he was thinking straight.'

Eve pulled her hair into a ponytail and used a band from around her wrist to tie it back.

'I think he knew me,' she said. 'Or had heard of me.'

Scott shook his head, his face still turned away.

'I know I'm different,' she said.

She'd said it many times before, but Scott had always convinced her otherwise.

'What do you mean?'

'Different,' she said. 'The way I think, the way I move. Even my eyes. I know I'm different.'

'You're not,' Scott said. 'I've known you all your life. You're as normal as I am.'

She smiled, and even looked as though she was about to laugh. 'You? Normal?'

'You see,' he said. 'What does normal even mean, anyway?'

Eve smiled weakly.

'You have your mother's eyes,' he said. 'They were brown with flecks of violet. Like yours.'

In her expression, he saw the desire to believe him. But it didn't last long. She opened her mouth to speak, then Gavin arrived beside them.

'All done,' he said, clapping his hands. He smiled at Eve, who ignored him and climbed onto the bus.

'Don't worry, kid,' Scott said, slapping Gavin on his back. 'Plenty more fish…'

'Is that meant to be funny?' Gavin said.

Scott led Gavin to the farmhouse to check for useful materials. They found candles, matches, lighters and various other useful knick-knacks, and put them in a rucksack.

In the living room, hanging on the wall, was a picture of a family: father, mother, son, daughter. Scott peered up at the ceiling: they were upstairs, lying on their beds, naked. He'd seen it too many times. He knew they were there.

Scott scanned the living room one last time. He found an old-fashioned parka, put it on and left, closely followed by Gavin, who had found a rifle and box of shells.

FOUR

SCOTT, sitting at the front of the bus, opened his eyes.

'Morning, sleepyhead,' George said, turning to look at Scott, his hands on the steering wheel, then turned back to watch the road.

'How much longer?' Scott asked.

George shrugged. 'Hard to say. Couple of hours.'

'We've been on the road forever.'

George raised a pointed finger. 'Edinburgh was your idea.'

'We need to keep on the move,' Scott said. 'Find more survivors.'

George nodded faintly. 'Eve still sleeping?'

Scott looked along the bus to the back seats, where a few of the younger children were huddled together, sleeping. 'She's sleeping for longer now.'

George smiled back at Scott in the rear-view mirror. 'She's growing up.'

Scott pursed his lips and remembered the day he took her from Dawn. 'She lost a tooth yesterday.'

'She did?' George asked, laughing to himself. 'Did the tooth fairy visit?'

Scott glanced towards the children. 'Well... I didn't know what to do.'

George appeared confused.

'Money is worthless now,' Scott said. 'No point giving her money.'

'Sure,' George said. 'But coins are shiny, and they look like they're worth something, don't they?'

Scott stroked his chin. 'I guess so.'

'So did you?'

'Then I thought about how the whole idea could disappear.'

'The tooth fairy?' George asked. 'Why would you want that?'

Scott shifted in his seat, sitting up straight. 'It's a lie.'

'A lie? It's not lying. Not really.'

Scott looked out of the window.

'Christ,' George said, 'talk about being a killjoy.'

'But what if we did?' Scott said. 'What if we changed things? Now? We could change it all – redesign the stories we tell our children. No more religion, no more fairy tales...'

'I'm with you on religion,' George said. 'But fairy tales, stories – they're all about imagination. Nothing wrong with that. She's only six...'

Scott continued to stare out of the window, watching the trees and hills rushing past. He'd thought about it so often over the years – how they were living in a place and time when they could choose to change all of it. There were only thousands of people left. If they could survive, they could change the narrative of the human race. For so long, religion, world politics and philosophies had influenced humanity. Now they could reset all of it. It both excited and scared him – that a few people would be in control of the stories children were told. In the Western world, so much literature, art and thought were centred on, and informed by, a Judeo-Christian narrative. Now that nearly everyone had been killed by Mathew and his Watchers, this knowledge and narrative had

THE VIOLET DAWN

been undermined. They had a blank slate upon which they could begin again. At no point in history had there been a moment like this.

'So you didn't give her anything for it?' George asked.

Scott ignored him. He saw Eve appear from her makeshift bed at the back of the bus. She ran along the gangway towards him.

'Good morning, beautiful,' Scott said, smiling, his arms open for her.

She ran into his arms and jumped onto his lap.

'Morning, Uncle George,' she said.

'Good morning. You sleep well, princess?'

'The tooth fairy,' she said, holding up a gold ring. 'She's been.'

'Has she?' George said, glancing at her. 'Wow! A gold ring.'

'Look,' Eve said, opening her mouth and showing George the gap in her teeth.

Scott kissed her on the top of the head. 'Uncle George is driving, sweetheart.'

She sat back and showed Scott the ring. 'Look, Daddy.'

It was a gold band Scott had had for a long time. He'd found it at Hassness House, in a jewellery box. It was the only ring he took. He didn't know why. But it played on his mind for days until he threaded it onto his little finger. It was something to do with jewellery, with decoration like that not being lost. It was an abstract thought, impossible to pin down rationally.

'You're a lucky girl,' Scott said. 'Here.' He took the ring from her and put it on her thumb.

'Does the tooth fairy take my tooth?' she asked, her face serious.

'Yes. She collects them from all the children.' Scott glanced up to see George smiling back at him.

'What does she do with them?' Eve asked.

Scott thought for a moment. 'She keeps them safe. Each tooth carries the memories of the boy or girl it came from. The tooth fairy has to keep all those memories safe.'

Eve opened her mouth wide to reveal the gap in the top row of her teeth. 'Really?' she managed to say.

Scott nodded, and this time he didn't look over at George.

'I'm going to show Jenny,' Eve said and hopped off Scott's lap. She stopped suddenly, turned, and looked questioningly at Scott. 'She is real, isn't she?'

Scott wasn't expecting the question, and wasn't expecting Eve's dark eyes to look at him so seriously. 'Yes,' he said. 'She's real.'

Eve stared. He held his breath. For a moment, he saw the shimmer of violet in her irises. He swallowed.

Eve bowed her head and examined the ring. He wanted to reassure her, but something stopped him. Again he thought about the truth and how if he was ever going to tell her, then it had to be in that moment. He could tell her the truth about everything. But he didn't understand what that would mean – for Eve, for him, for what remained of humanity. Maybe the story of the tooth fairy had survived because it served a purpose. He couldn't remember the tooth fairy visiting him. He tried to remember, but there was nothing there. He remembered the sensation of a tooth wobbling, his tongue pushing against it, but that was all.

'She's real,' he said.

'Cross your heart?'

'And hope to die.'

Eve smiled and hugged him again before running to the back of the bus.

'She's real, then,' George said. 'The tooth fairy.'

Scott didn't look at him. 'She's real,' he said. 'For now. She's real.'

FIVE

SCOTT WATCHED as Eve manoeuvred the bus through the narrow roads of north Wales, all the time glancing around for any threats. She was the best driver and hadn't once had an accident.

There were other times, though, when Scott convinced himself – usually when Eve did something human, like drop a cup, or say the wrong thing and blush – that what Mathew had told him about her seemed ridiculous. Mathew had made it sound as though Eve would be different in ways that were obvious. That she was half human, half artificial intelligence should have been obvious. But she was the same as everyone else. At least, she was the same as everyone else in that she had her own quirks, her own personality, and was unique. Unlike anyone else. During these moments of fallibility, Scott felt his chest swell with relief. It made sense that Mathew would lie to him. After all, his whole life was a lie.

But there were other days, other moments, that unsettled him. Like watching Eve drive the bus. Those moments reminded him of what Mathew had told him. The way she scanned the road ahead, or reached for the gear stick, or maintained an exact speed, made his chest tighten. It was the exactness of her movements as though everything was being processed, mechanised. It also made him think when she warned him there was a scent in the air she didn't recognise, or had a feeling that made her avoid driving to certain places. He didn't know exactly what it meant, that Eve was the product of AI design. But now and then he saw what he considered were the advantages – such as the way she looked people in the eye when she spoke to them, or how she fell asleep at night, within seconds, as though her mind was untroubled. Sleep for Scott, on the other hand, on the days he saw the truth in what Mathew said, was far more difficult to find.

Eve pulled the bus into a car park outside a lodge in Snowdonia. She and Elidi were the first ones off the bus. Places like hotels and lodges were sometimes free of bodies, so Scott was hopeful when he entered the first building. Most people had been at home when the Rapture happened; few people had ignored the date. It had been so long ago, yet – somehow – the bodies remained as they had been on the day of the Rapture.

Eve and Elidi checked one of the other lodges. Scott nodded over at Eve as he opened the door. Part of him hoped it was locked. It opened, and he pushed it open. Inside, he smelled the mustiness of a building that had been unoccupied for two decades.

The lodge was made up of seven different buildings. Only one of them housed a body: the smallest building was home to a woman who lay on the floor, still dressed. Maybe she hadn't believed the Rapture was going to happen – there were some who didn't. Maybe it was more a case of not wanting to believe it. Elidi closed the door, telling the children to stay away from that building; they nodded, accustomed to such imperative, non-negotiable commands.

Sarah killed two sheep with a rifle. Helped by Manpreet, she dragged them back to the lodge. Eve and Gavin had foraged through the gardens at the rear of the lodge and stumbled across an overgrown allotment. They found self-seeded potatoes and rhubarb that was growing wild. There were two wood burners in the kitchen, and Eve set about preparing baked potatoes. The smell of them cooking filled the lodge and enticed everyone into the kitchen.

After they'd eaten, Scott poured glasses of whisky from a bottle he'd found in the small bar in the building furthest from the road. It was the original sort – before they'd added whatever chemicals they used to add. It was the first time either Eve or Gavin had tried it.

Eve winced. 'What is that? Has it gone bad?'

Scott smiled. 'That's how it's supposed to taste.'

'Why would you want to drink that?' Gavin asked, holding the glass at arm's length.

'You get used to it,' Scott said, taking a long drink and pouring another.

Eve peered into her glass.

'Down it,' Scott said. 'You'll enjoy the effect, if not the taste.'

Eve and Gavin glanced at one another and nodded.

Scott counted. 'One, two, three.'

They downed the whisky. Both coughed and spluttered.

'Good, huh?' Scott said.

Gavin held his throat. 'God, no!'

Eve closed her eyes tight, snarled, and shook her head.

After three more shots of whisky each, Eve and Gavin convinced Scott to play cards. They played for matchsticks. Scott was down to his last one when he noticed Gavin was asleep, lying on the floor next to Eve, who had won every other matchstick.

'He loves you,' Scott said, nodding at Gavin.

Eve blushed and blinked slowly, the whisky and tiredness slowing her movements.

'Be kind to him,' he said. 'Be clear that you don't love him back, but be kind. He's a good kid.'

She looked as though she was about to say something, then stopped and nodded.

Eve won the last matchstick. Scott lay down on the floor, using a cushion he'd taken from a settee for his head. He felt a blanket fall across his legs and chest, and noticed she'd done the same for Gavin.

'I'm different,' she said.

Scott had closed his eyes and didn't want to open them.

'Dad?' she said. 'I'm different, aren't I?'

Scott opened his eyes. 'I've told you. No more than anyone else.'

'I'm different. I know I am. The way I think. The way I behave. It's not the same as everyone else.' She glanced down at Gavin. 'I don't think the same way.'

'You do. And how would you know if you didn't?'

She folded her arms around her legs and tucked them in close to her chest, resting her chin on her knees. 'I feel like I'm missing something – something Gavin has, that you have.'

Scott sat up opposite her. He swallowed hard.

'You know what I mean?' she asked.

'It's the whisky,' Scott said.

She shook her head. 'No. I think the whisky helps me see it. But I've always known it. It's the way people describe the way they think and feel. Sometimes I don't recognise it in myself.'

Relief surged through him at the thought of being able to tell her everything.

She stared at him, her pupils dilated from the whisky, a ring of violet shining around each one, crystalline.

'You've always been honest with me,' she said. 'You always will, won't you?'

He swallowed again, but something stuck in his throat. He coughed, making Gavin stir in his sleep. 'Of course.'

She stared at him, her pupils shrinking and the violet rings shimmering back to the brown they were for most of the time.

There was still time. He knew that. There was still time to tell her. 'There is something,' he said.

'Did I win?' Gavin mumbled, sitting up.

'What?' Eve asked Scott, her brow furrowed. 'What is it?'

Scott looked at Gavin, then back at Eve. 'It can wait.'

Eve was clearly disappointed but nodded.

Scott placed his palm on his chest. 'That whisky,' he said. 'It's not good for you.' He glanced at Eve one last time before leaving the room to find a bed for the night. Already he regretted not telling her – a moment had passed and he was annoyed with himself for not taking it.

SIX

EVE OPENED HER EYES. She was cold, and her head throbbed. The whisky. She rubbed her face and eyes. Gavin was lying on his back, snoring. There was no sign of Scott, but then she remembered him leaving the room. Outside it was still dark. She heard wind and the sound of rain skittering through the trees and against the window. She reached for a blanket from the chair beside her, but a hushed voice made her stop moving and hold her breath. Tilting her head, she listened. There was a constant whisper. She stood and walked wearily over to Gavin. The whispering grew louder, rising and falling like speech but indistinguishable as individual words. She checked on Gavin, who was sleeping. The whispering stopped, and she waited. It started again, travelling along the landing from one direction from a door at the far end of the narrow corridor. She padded quietly out of the room, her socked feet silent. The door the whispering was coming from was ajar. Inside the room, Scott was asleep in bed, wrapped up in a duvet, extra blankets thrown across him. She edged inside the room, ready to wake him and ask whether he heard the whispering too. It was coming from beneath the bed. She dropped to her knees to look. A rucksack. She lifted her head to check on Scott again, who was still sleeping, then reached beneath the bed and pulled out the bag. Whatever was inside was heavy. She opened the zip and peered in. A black box. With a shaking hand she touched it and felt a shock, a violent surge in her stomach as though she'd fallen into a fierce river. She let go and held a fist to her chest, breathing deeply.

She waited, staring at the rucksack. The whispering had stopped. Her head spun with what it meant. It had been an unpleasant experience, but also exhilarating. The room was quiet except for Scott's slow, deep breathing. She peered inside the rucksack again. This time she held the black box and pulled it towards her chest.

A blur of movement...

Pulled through to somewhere...

Falling ... accelerating...

And then a voice.

'Eve?'

'Yes,' she said – or thought.

Everything was dark apart from the light shining through an archway. The light grew brighter until she had to raise an arm to shield her eyes. She opened her eyes again. It was dark. A pair of eyes, violet like her own, peered back at her. A man holding a revolver. In front of him was a row of men, women and children, all on their knees. The man with violet eyes held a revolver to the back of their heads, then shot each one. They fell to the ground.

Eve couldn't move.

A second pair of violet eyes, then a third and a fourth.

Eve turned and faced the four silhouettes. She saw them breathing slowly, their shoulders lifting and falling. One of them shifted their weight from one leg to the other and turned to look at others.

She heard whispering from somewhere far away, but couldn't make out what the voices were saying.

The dark figures stared back at her. She closed her eyes and straightened her shoulders in defiance. She squeezed her eyes shut, then found herself back in Scott's room. Her heart pounded and her mouth was dry. The sound of wind and rain outside replaced the whispering. She shoved the box into the rucksack and pushed it back under the bed.

She left the room as quietly as she had entered, taking her time to walk across the landing, back to the room where Gavin slept. She lay on the settee and reached for the blanket, curled up and closed her eyes. Remembering, she saw each person falling forward, the revolver firing into the back of their skulls. Then she saw the four figures, their violet eyes peering back at her. Scott knew the truth, she was sure of it. And no matter how much he'd reassured her, something told her he was lying to her. She deserved to know who she was! The more time that passed, the more different she felt to everyone else. How could a box, an inanimate thing, make her see something like that? It could have been real — as though what she was seeing was actually happening in that moment but in a different place. She wanted to go back and try again, but something in the back of her mind told her to stay away from it. She opened her eyes and saw the room through a violet hue – the colour she'd tried to ignore all her life. But there was no ignoring it any longer.

SEVEN

SCOTT OPENED his eyes and squinted at the morning light streaming through the curtain-less window. His head was sore. He kicked away the duvet, swung his legs over the side of the bed and sat up.

'Good morning.' A woman's voice.

He turned, something in his neck grinding. 'It is?'

It was Elidi. 'You're not going to Liverpool?'

Scott inhaled and stretched. 'No.'

'There could be others,' she said. 'We've spent so long on the run, maybe it's time to turn back and look for people who we can help and who might help us.'

He rubbed the back of his neck. 'Something doesn't feel right. The way the Watcher asked about them.'

'Just think about it,' she said. 'Maybe now's the time to stick together. There's safety in numbers.'

Elidi walked into the room and sat on the bed. She'd been the only one who would spend any length of time with him. Scott waited for her to speak, suspecting, from the way she was sitting, she had something important to tell him.

Scott turned to the side. 'What is it?'

Elidi got up to look out of the window. She took a deep breath and gently bit her bottom lip. She was younger than Scott, in her thirties, but there was something in her demeanour that everyone recognised as authority.

'It's Eve,' she said.

Scott knew where the conversation was going, and turned away. He heard her move around the bed to his side, where she sat.

'You need to tell me,' she said.

Scott stared at the floor between his bare feet. 'Tell you what?'

He watched her out of the corner of his eye. She rubbed her left arm, then arranged the collar of her dress.

'I don't fully understand what's happening. But I know there's something going on with her. For as long as I've known the two of you, I've—'

'I don't know what you mean,' Scott said, standing and moving to the window.

'There's no time to go through all this now. I want you to be honest with me. Honest with her.'

Outside, the sky was clear, but the distant mountains were hazy. Already he felt relief – the same as when he had been on the verge of telling Eve everything. He longed to unburden himself, talk to someone about what he'd been told.

'I've heard rumours,' Elidi said.

'What rumours?'

'Just rumours. I saw what Eve did to that Watcher. I saw the way you looked at her after she did it. Like you wanted to stop her but knew you wouldn't be able to. And her eyes...'

He'd kept it to himself for so long, he didn't know where to begin.

'I'm not her father,' he said before thinking it through. He couldn't look at her.

'I'd guessed that,' she said.

Already he was relieved. And it felt easier than it had in the past to tell her everything. She smiled warmly. He'd not seen her smile like that before – certainly not at him.

'Did you know her mother?' she asked.

Scott nodded. 'Dawn. She died young – only weeks before the Rapture. I tried to help her, but I couldn't. Mathew ... did things to young women. I can guess what he was doing. But there was more to it. I don't know what exactly, but Eve ... she's the product of whatever Mathew was doing.'

Elidi intertwined her fingers, deep in thought.

'Are these the rumours you've heard?' Scott asked her.

'Sort of. I've heard there are others like Eve, who are half human, half ... half something else.'

Scott nodded slowly, watching Elidi for a sign he could tell her more.

'Does she know?' Elidi asked.

Scott shook his head. 'I haven't told her. But she suspects she's different.'

'You have to tell her.'

'But tell her what exactly? That not only am I not her father, but she's the result of Mathew's experiment?'

It was clear Elidi was troubled.

'Believe me,' Scott went on, 'I've wanted to tell her everything. And I've come close several times. But I can't. I've never been able to do it.'

'What do you know exactly?'

Eve came into view through the window. She was with Elidi's son, Daker, who was kicking a football against a wall.

'Only what Mathew has told me. And Samuel – but he made little sense.'

'What did Mathew tell you?'

'That she's a different sort of human. He called her a New Human.'

Elidi waited for him to continue.

'The AI is inside her,' he went on. 'Parts of her are controlled by nanotechnology. She will reach an optimum age, then stop ageing. She appears to have a connection with electrical apparatus and machines. I've seen it several times. She just knows automatically how to work them. Like driving – she learned so easily. When she's pushed, under stress, it comes out. When she was a baby, she killed Samuel, a Watcher who was threatening to kill her. It happened in a flash, but I saw it in her eyes. She's human, but also …'

Through the window they watched Eve helping Daker stand, having fallen.

'She's human, Scott. Anyone can see that. But if what you've been told is true, she'll soon reach an age where the ageing process the rest of us experience might not happen for her. She'll know something is different.'

Scott nodded weakly.

'You have to talk to her.'

Scott recalled the night before and the moment he nearly told her. Maybe that was the whisky. Now, he couldn't imagine how he might tell her. 'No. Not yet. It's not time.'

Elidi sighed. 'Why? Why not now?'

'I'm not sure. There'll be time for that. But it's not now.'

'She deserves to know the truth.'

'The truth?' Scott asked. 'When has the truth helped any of us? The truth about our dates … the truth about the AI …

the truth about the Rapture. We'd have been better off not knowing any of it.'

Elidi didn't speak, but he felt her eyes on him.

'I'll tell her. When the time's right.'

'You know what I've learned in all this, Scott? It's that all we have is the truth. If we have any chance of starting again, we have to do things differently. And I think the one thing we have to change is, we have to stop lying to one another. Even if we believe it's for the best. I've learned that it's never for the best ... not in the long run. It might hurt, it might feel like the wrong thing to do. But it's not. Tell her the truth. We'll help her deal with whatever happens. Then she'll know she can trust you. Trust all of us.'

Outside, Eve played with Daker.

'I will,' he said.

'When?' she urged.

'I will,' he said again.

Elidi walked to the door, then stopped and turned towards him. 'I've known you a long time. I've never thought of you as a coward.'

It hurt. Not only because of what it meant, but because it reminded him of Freya, who'd told him the same thing.

Elidi left the room. A hundred words flashed through his mind but he couldn't decide on one of them.

EIGHT

SCOTT WATCHED Eve open her present. It was her seventh birthday.

It was too cruel that her birthday should be the same date as her mum's death. She didn't know this, but Scott remembered that day clearly. Twenty-fourth of February.

He hadn't meant to lie to begin with; it sort of happened in its own time. Somehow, Eve had invented her own version of what had happened to her mother, and Scott just played along. His vagueness fed her inventions.

'What is it?' she asked, smiling, her cheeks flushed.

'It's a paint set.'

'Paint set,' she said, nodding. She unrolled the tube of paper and placed the paints on top.

'Your mum,' Scott said. 'She used to paint – all the time. I wish I had some of her paintings to show you. I know where they are. One day we'll see them.' He remembered Hassness House and Dawn's paintings on the walls in her room.

Eve sat up straight. 'Will you show me how to paint?'

'I don't think I can paint myself,' he said. 'I can show you how to mix the colours, though.'

Eve frowned. 'Mix them?'

'Sure,' Scott said. 'If you mix certain colours together, they make other colours.'

'Show me,' she said, leaning closer to the paints.

Scott cleared the table of wrapping paper and laid out a sheet of the paper.

'We need some water,' he said, pointing to a bottle over by the sink.

Eve hopped off her chair and ran over to the sink to grab the bottle.

Scott opened the paint set. Taking the bottle from Eve, he dipped the brush into the water.

'We need to make the paintbrush wet.'

Eve nodded, kneeling on her chair, her elbows on the table, her face hovering above the paper.

Scott rubbed the brush against the block of yellow paint and then transferred the colour to the paper. Eve smiled back at him.

'Yellow,' she said.

Scott nodded. 'Then you wash your brush in the water.' He watched the yellow paint colour the water. 'Then we add some blue.'

Eve watched the end of the paintbrush rub against the block of blue paint. Scott swiped the end of the brush left and right beneath the streak of yellow.

'Now watch when we mix the colours.' The brush moved up to the yellow paint, and he mixed in the blue. 'You see?'

Eve covered her mouth, her eyes wide.

'Green,' Scott said.

Eve shook her head. 'That's magic.'

'Can you guess how we'd make pink?'

'We can make pink?'

Scott nodded. 'Can you guess which colours we need?'

Eve scrutinised the circular blocks of paint, then the paper. 'Red.'

'That's right.' *He could see she didn't want to guess the next colour. 'And white.' He handed her the brush.*

'Me?' she said.

'Have a go.'

She shook her head. 'No, I might get it wrong.'

'It's painting,' he said. 'You can't get it wrong. It's fun, that's all.'

She took the brush from him and stared at it. 'What was Mum's favourite colour?'

Her question caught him by surprise. He thought back to the short time they'd spent together at Hassness House. Looking back, even though Scott knew Dawn had little time remaining, he remembered it as a peaceful time. Her paintings were of the sky and the harsh winter landscapes in the Lake District. She'd also painted – he tried to remember – her mother twice.

'I remember her using a very dark blue for the sky,' he said. 'It was almost black, but you could tell it was blue.'

Eve rubbed the blue block of paint and wiped her brush across the top of the paper.

'The sky,' she said, then washed her brush and used the black paint. Having turned the end of her brush black, she mixed it with the blue. The paint turned a dirty colour, not a deep pure blue at all.

'Like this?' she asked.

'That's it. Keep playing with the colours.'

Scott left her at the table and walked over to a chair beside the fire. He picked up the hardback copy of Brave New World he'd found in the library in Birmingham. He opened it and the smell of old books wafted up. Now, whenever he took a book in his hands, the fear that at some point they might all be lost made him sad. The thought that either books or humans would no longer be around meant all that work, all that knowledge and creativity, would be wasted. If there were no humans left to read the books mankind had produced, what was any of it for? He glanced over at Eve, working busily with her paintbrush. He read to her every night, hoping she would want to read herself. She enjoyed the stories he read to her, but he could never tell if she enjoyed him being there with her, or whether she just enjoyed hearing the stories. She had quickly learned to read, but he'd not found her once reading herself.

He reread the opening of the novel.

After a while, his eyes beginning to close, he heard Eve cry out in frustration.

'What is it?'

Eve had thrown down her brush and crossed her arms. 'It's not the way I want it.'

'It takes time and practice,' he said.

She shook her head. 'This isn't the way things look.'

'What do you mean?'

Eve grabbed her paper and walked over to Scott to show him. 'Look,' she said, pointing to her painting. 'This is you. But it doesn't look like you.'

'Evie,' he said, 'that's not how painting works. What you paint doesn't have to look like the real world.'

She stared at him, frowning.

'In fact, some of the best paintings people have made are paintings that don't look like the real world at all. Some artists paint what they see in their heads.'

Eve shook her head slowly and turned to her own painting. 'I don't like it.'

'Then try another one. You might like that one.'

'Do you like it?' she asked him.

'For a first painting, I think it's amazing.'

She stared at him, her eyes turning violet, her shoulders raised. 'Liar!'

'Eve?' he said, reaching for her. 'Don't use that word.'

She took a step backwards and threw the painting to the ground. 'I can tell when you're lying,' she said. 'My painting is no good – and you said it was.'

'Painting isn't like that,' he said. He thought for a moment, trying to think of the best way to explain. But it was too late.

'I hate painting!' she said and ran out of the room.

She was stubborn about certain things, and he knew, as he picked up the painting, that it would be her one and only effort. He tidied up the table and hid the paints and brushes away in a drawer.

He checked outside on Eve, who sat on the swing at the bottom of the garden. He thought back to when they'd arrived at this house with everyone else. Always the first one to enter, he'd found twin boys, teenagers, with their mother and father, naked on their beds. He saw the four of them as paintings, their bodies laid out, one beside the other, all dead, all still.

NINE

THE MORE ELIDI'S words played over and over in his head, the more frustrated Scott became. He wasn't a coward. He'd done everything he could to protect Eve – to protect all of them. And what she'd said about him not going to Liverpool also bothered him, and now he couldn't be sure whether he didn't want to go because he was afraid it was a trap, or because he was being stubborn.

The next morning, Scott found Gavin asleep. He kicked the duvet covering Gavin's legs. 'Time to rise and shine.'

Gavin jumped and sat up, holding his head, then fell back down again. 'What the hell!'

Scott smirked. 'That'll be the whisky. You shouldn't drink it.'

He placed a steaming cup of tea on the table, next to the pack of cards they'd used the night before. Scott shuffled the cards, remembering how every shuffled deck, because of the odds involved, was unique. He placed the shuffled deck on the table.

'I need to talk to you,' Scott said.

Gavin reached for the tea and sipped it, gazing seriously

at Scott. Gavin's eagerness always frustrated Scott, for reasons he couldn't understand. But even now, knowing what he needed from Gavin, Scott wanted the young man to show more ... something like doubt or suspicion. But there was none of that in the young man's demeanour. Ever.

'It's important that you listen carefully. You'll be the only other person who knows this.'

Gavin nodded.

'You don't know what it is yet,' Scott said. Already he was regretting his decision. Maybe Gavin wasn't the best person to tell. What he was asking of him could be too much. But if he told no one and something happened to him, then Mathew would find it, eventually. He had little choice.

'Whatever you need,' Gavin said and sat up straight, pushing away the duvet.

Scott pursed his lips and inhaled. He took the rucksack he'd dropped by the table and opened it, taking out the black box.

Gavin stared at it, then at Scott, and then back at the black box. 'What is it?'

Scott couldn't believe he was about to tell Gavin everything. 'I've had this for nearly twenty years. I've often thought about destroying it.' He turned it over in his hands. Whenever he held the box, its weight and solidity amazed him. 'But I wouldn't know how to.' He handed it to Gavin. 'If anything happens to me, I need to know there'll be someone else to look after it.'

'It's heavy. Really heavy. What is it?'

'The AI,' Scott said.

Gavin let go of the box, letting it fall onto the duvet. 'The what?'

'When I destroyed the AI, it asked me to take this with

me. Otherwise it would have fallen into Mathew's hands. And neither the AI nor I wanted that.'

'The AI? The only things I've heard of the AI are bad. I don't understand it, but I know it's evil.'

'It's not evil. It was Mathew who wielded its power.'

'And this is it?'

'A part of it, at least. It contains the AI's fundamental consciousness, or the ingredients to bring it back. I'm not entirely sure how it works.'

'Get rid of it!' Gavin said, staring at it with wide eyes.

'How?' Scott asked. 'I don't know how to destroy it. Look at it.'

'Bury it. Drop it in the ocean. Anything. Just get rid of it.'

'And what if Mathew finds it? He'd be able to create an AI far more powerful, capable of tracking every surviving human.'

Gavin shook his head, standing and retreating as far away from the box as he could.

'We'll do whatever it takes,' Scott said, 'to make sure it doesn't end up in Mathew's hands.' He lifted the box, examining it closely. 'But what if we can use it ourselves? For good?'

'No,' Gavin said.

Scott had not seen Gavin behave this way before.

'In the back of my mind, I've been wondering how we can use it for good, to help humanity rebuild, to lead to goodness and prosperity for everyone.'

'No,' Gavin said again, but louder. 'Don't think like that! The AI will manipulate us. Or there'll be someone like Mathew, ready to use it for all the wrong reasons.' Gavin pointed at the box. 'We have to destroy it.'

Scott could see there was no use trying to reason with him. 'Okay, we will.'

Gavin's forehead creased. 'Now!'

'When we work out how best to do it.'

Gavin stared at the black box. 'What will we do with it now?'

'I need you to look after it,' Scott said.

Fear came back into Gavin's expression.

'It will be okay,' Scott said. 'It's just while I'm in Liverpool.'

Gavin shook his head slowly. 'You said you weren't going.'

'I've changed my mind. We need to help them. It's time we stopped running and instead tried to find safety in numbers.'

As if it was a black hole, the black box pulled at their attention and their bodies.

'You can do it,' Scott said. 'I won't be long. I'm taking Eve with me, but I need someone I can trust to look after this while I'm gone. It can never fall into Mathew's hands. Ever.'

Now Gavin nodded. 'Ever,' he said. 'But I want to come with you.'

'No. I need you here, to look after everyone else, and to look after this.'

Gavin shook his head. 'No. You'll need me there.'

'I need you here more.' Scott slid the black box back into the rucksack. 'I need you to find somewhere to hide this.'

Gavin walked back and forth, then stopped. 'I know where we can hide it.' He grabbed the rucksack and led Scott out of the room, down the stairs and into an unused bedroom on the ground floor. 'I noticed these floorboards when we arrived.' He lifted the floorboards, revealing a large space beneath. Gavin climbed down into it with the rucksack. Scott listened to him shuffling around. Finally, he emerged, his hair, face and clothes dusty.

'Good hiding place,' Scott said.

Gavin said nothing as he lifted himself up.

'Keep it safe while we're gone. We leave tomorrow morning.'

Gavin replaced the floorboards. 'Does Eve know about this?'

'No,' Scott said quickly. 'No one else knows. Only you and me. Don't tell anyone.'

Gavin sighed and nodded reluctantly.

'Promise me?' Scott asked.

'I promise,' Gavin said, staring at the floor.

Scott remembered an Edgar Allan Poe story about a dead body hidden beneath floorboards. Then he remembered what Elidi had said about the importance of truth. But the truth was not a luxury anyone had when the world was ending.

TEN

IN WINTER, Eve thought, the nights were so long that the daylight seemed temporary, hardly there at all.

Scott had told her they were going to Liverpool the following day. The thought that she might be hours away from finding new people both intrigued and worried her.

She watched Gavin fan out his cards, then stare at them. He'd been behaving strangely all day. 'What's wrong with you?' she asked.

Gavin stared at his cards, apparently not having heard her.

Eve's brow wrinkled. 'Hey,' she said, nudging Gavin with her foot.

Gavin shook himself awake. 'My go?'

'Yeah!' Eve said. 'What's wrong?'

'Nothing. You should get some sleep.'

'I'll be fine,' she said. 'Another hand or two.' She pointed her winning cards at him.

Gavin shrugged. 'What's the point? You win every time anyway.'

'Then concentrate. What's up with you today?' She shuffled the cards, dealt, and placed the rest of the cards in a neat stack on the floor. 'You and Dad have been up to something, haven't you?'

Gavin gave her a puzzled look.

'I've seen you together. Something strange is going on.'

'I don't know what you mean. Your turn.' He nodded at her cards.

She took a card, then placed another on the carpet. When she was around Gavin, she had felt nothing other than friendship for him. And he was a good friend – one she could trust. Gavin was reliable. But that impression of him was shifting. Her dad had lied to her – for reasons she knew he believed were for the best. She'd never had to worry about trying to read Gavin's mind. He took a card and placed another down on the floor.

'I trust you,' she said. 'More than anyone else here. Even Dad.'

He appeared to be as surprised as she was. But she'd meant it, and she hoped Gavin knew that.

'I trust you too,' he said. 'More than anyone.'

There was an apology in his words.

'So why does it feel like you know something you're not telling me?'

Gavin bowed his head. 'You said you trusted me.'

'I do.'

'Then you need to trust me now.'

She'd not seen this side of him before and didn't want to challenge him. He spoke with a maturity that suited him. He stared at her, his eyes serious, his mouth a straight, fixed line. His arms and shoulders were more substantial, somehow, and his stubble shimmered in the moonlight coming in through the window.

'Your turn,' he said, smiling.

She recalled the conversation she'd had with her dad – about how Gavin had feelings for her. She should tell him how she felt – that she just wanted to be friends. It would be cruel to lead him on and make him believe there would ever be anything more between them.

'Eve,' he said. 'Your turn.'

She put her cards down, knelt, crawled across the space between them and kissed him. His gulp was audible. She opened her eyes and pulled back so she was sitting on her heels. Why did people kiss? She had some notion of how it should have felt, but she'd never felt the desire to kiss a boy – or a girl. It was something else that had made her feel different. She wanted to try it, to know why people enjoyed it. But she had felt nothing. And almost immediately, she regretted doing it.

'What ... what was that for?'

She touched her lips with a finger. It was her first kiss, and undoubtedly Gavin's too. 'I'm not sure. Should I not have? You're my best friend and I wanted to thank you.'

Gavin's brow furrowed deeply. 'What for?'

'For looking out for me. You always have.'

She felt Gavin staring at her as she retreated, picked up her cards and fanned them out. As she put down a card, she knew she'd confused things between them.

'Your eyes,' he said. 'They sort of ... changed colour. After you kissed me...'

'Dad says I have Mum's eyes.'

Gavin nodded, still in a daze.

'It's your turn,' she said.

Slowly, his eyes dropped to scan his cards. He selected a card and placed it on top of the overturned deck. He took another from the pile beside it and added it to his hand.

Eve took the card he'd just put down and fanned her cards out on the carpet.

'You win again,' he said.

'It was about a box, wasn't it?' she said. 'A black box.'

Gavin held his breath, his eyes still fixed on her cards.

'You don't have to say anything,' she said. 'I know it was.'

'Scott made me promise.'

'Have you held it?' she asked him. 'The box.'

He nodded.

'And did ... did anything happen when you held it?'

He appeared confused. 'What do you mean?'

The look in his eye told her he was being honest. He'd not had the same experience she'd had.

'It's the AI, isn't it?' she asked.

Gavin looked away again, towards the doorway. 'Is this why you kissed me? To get me to tell you?'

'No,' she said, and meant it. But now he'd said it, she couldn't help thinking that might have been the reason. 'No,' she said again. 'I wasn't thinking about that.'

Gavin was clearly hurt. He dropped the cards, then stood. 'I'm going to bed.'

'I'm sorry,' she said. 'I didn't mean for you to think ... I didn't do that to...'

'It's okay,' he said. 'I'll see you in the morning before you go.'

She got to her feet, wanting to stand in his way, but it was too late. Again, she noticed his broadening shoulders and lean arms and wondered what kind of man he would become – and then, what kind of woman she would become.

ELEVEN

SCOTT SAW Eve fall from the top of the tree, down through the branches, and land on the ground with a thud. She didn't move at first. There was a shocked silence. Her legs and arms were angled strangely. He ran towards the tree, already working out what he needed to do – find a surgical-machine and, with George's help, fix her. Her face was contorted with pain, her eyes a deep violet.

'It's okay,' he said, dropping to his knees. He went to touch her, then saw a pointed branch imbedded in her calf, buried deep. He glanced back to the house.

'George!' he shouted.

There was the sound of a door opening behind him.

'Find George!' he shouted.

He saw she couldn't breathe – her face reddened, her hand reached for her throat, then her stomach.

'It'll be okay,' he said, and brushed hair away from her face. It was all he could do.

After what felt like forever, George was beside him.

'I need you to take tiny breaths,' George told her in a calm voice. 'I know it hurts, but you're winded and you need to get

some air back into your lungs.' He laid a hand on her cheek. *'That's it, tiny little bits of air.'*

'What do we do?' Scott asked.

George examined her leg. 'I need you to get the surgical kit.'

Scott got to his feet and ran into the house.

The rest of the day was a blur. Scott was helpless the whole time, and felt solace only when George asked him to do something, however menial.

Later that day, Eve lay in bed, asleep, her leg bandaged. Her arm was broken, and countless grazes and bruises marked her hip, chest and face.

'We need to get her to a surgical-machine in the morning,' George said. *'I've given her painkillers for now. But I need help with her arm – the radius.'*

Scott watched Eve sleeping.

'I remember what happened,' George said.

Scott immediately knew what he was talking about. They hadn't spoken about it – perhaps because neither of them wanted to consider it.

'I remember that surgical-machine killing Samuel,' George said. 'I remember the colour of her eyes. Like earlier, when she'd fallen from the tree. Did you see them?'

Scott couldn't look at him but nodded.

'I know she's older, but there's a chance, if she feels threatened, that she'll react in the same way.'

Scott shook his head. 'No. She won't hurt us.'

George didn't look at him, but Scott knew he was unconvinced.

They took it in turns watching her through the night. In the early morning, Scott, sitting in the chair next to Eve's bed, was nudged awake by George.

'She's awake,' George whispered.

Scott sat up in the chair. He saw straight away that Eve's face had healed – there was no signs of bruising, cuts or grazes.

George didn't look surprised. The look he gave Scott communicated what they both knew but hadn't acknowledged: that she was different.

'What happened?' Eve asked, taking a cup of water from Scott.

'You fell out of the tree.'

Eve's brow furrowed as she tried to remember. 'I felt dizzy,' she said. 'I looked down at the ground and it spun and my stomach felt funny and then ... then I don't remember.'

'Scared of heights, huh?' George said, laying a hand on her arm. 'Me too.'

George examined her and confirmed that not only had her broken arm healed itself, but that the wound made by the tree branch was no longer there.

'Am I going to be okay?' she asked, pushing the bed covers aside. She swung her legs over the side of the bed and jumped down.

'I think you'll be just fine,' George said.

They watched her leave the room with no sign of injury.

'What do we tell the others?' George asked.

'I'm not sure. Have you ever seen anything like that before?' Scott asked.

George shook his head. 'I remember what Samuel said about her. About her being ... what did he call her? An abomination?'

Scott recalled hearing Samuel use precisely that word.

George sighed. 'We've not talked about it a lot, I know. But I think it's time we started. What did he mean exactly?'

'I'm not sure,' Scott said. 'But it has something to do with what we've just seen.'

'And her eyes?' George asked.

'It happens when she's stressed, or feels under threat.'

'I remember how the surgical-machine behaved,' George said. 'The way it killed Samuel. She did that, didn't she?'

Scott nodded and checked around the room before lowering his voice. 'Mathew experimented on pregnant women. Modifying foetuses so they were infused with the AI. I'm guessing her DNA, combined with AI and nanotechnology, means her body mends at a much faster rate.'

They both stared at the bed in which Eve had been lying. The bed sheets were pulled back, her pillows leaning against the headboard.

'Faster?' George said. 'You're not wrong there.'

'We'll tell the others it wasn't as bad as we thought it was.'

'Some of them already know there's something ... different about her.'

Scott knew it too. It was in their looks, in the words they used – and didn't use. 'Maybe we'll have to tell people.'

George shook his head. 'That's a bad idea.'

Scott waited.

'She's different,' George said. 'And no matter how much we try, people won't like or trust her. People don't like people who are different.'

Scott wanted to argue, but deep down he knew George was right. He'd articulated something so simple and obvious: people mistrusted those who were not the same as them.

TWELVE

THE NEXT MORNING, Scott found Elidi waiting with her son by the 4×4 Eve had found and loaded, ready to go. Daker ran off towards his football.

'You think there'll be people there?' Elidi asked him. 'In Liverpool?'

'We'll find out.'

She bit her lip. 'I'm sorry. About what I said.'

Scott recalled the word 'coward'. He raised his hand and waved away her apology.

She brushed strands of hair behind her ear. 'It's just…'

'It's fine.'

Scott opened the door and placed a bag on the back seat.

He watched Elidi look over at her son with a worried expression.

'What is it?' he asked.

She shook her head. 'Nothing.'

Scott waited, wondering what she was thinking.

'What if you're right,' she said, 'and it is a trap?'

'Well, we can't leave them there. Like you said, if there are others, we need to stick together.'

THE VIOLET DAWN

Elidi touched his arm. 'Be careful.'

The touch and her expression confused him. Because she was so much younger than he was, he'd not even thought that she might like him in that way. Scott remembered Elidi's husband. The day before, when Scott had spoken to Elidi, he'd seen something different in her manner but thought he was mistaken. Seeing the same look again confirmed it. She let go of his arm.

'Did you tell her?' she asked.

Scott sighed. 'No.'

Elidi crossed her arms and nodded, but without the disappointment she'd shown the day before.

'I will,' Scott said. 'When the time's right.'

Again, she nodded.

He didn't want to have the same argument. 'There are still a few things I need.' He excused himself and walked back inside and into his bedroom, all the time feeling the weight of her stare.

'Are we ready?' Eve asked, coming into his room.

Scott checked all around. 'All set.'

'Have you seen Gavin?' she asked. 'I can't find him.'

'Not this morning. You have a late night?'

'Not really,' she said.

'I've not seen him,' Scott said, opening a drawer and taking out a revolver. He pushed it into his coat pocket.

Eve left the room and Scott went back out to the 4×4 to check one last time he had everything they'd need.

'Be safe,' he heard a voice say. He turned to see Elidi with an arm around Daker's shoulder.

'We will,' Scott said and smiled reassuringly.

Her smile in return was weak but warm. She let go of Daker and again glanced at Scott before going back inside.

Scott checked his revolver, then the back seat for the

53

rifles. He waited, looking around now and then for Eve. He recalled the conversation he'd had the day before with Gavin and figured it was this conversation that had made him disappear. Perhaps the boy was thinking about what they'd said. But he could trust Gavin to do the right thing. Eve appeared in a window on the ground floor, then on the landing on the second floor. She seemed to be looking for Gavin. Scott climbed into the passenger seat and opened the window. Wales was so green, he couldn't get used to it. Everywhere he looked, there were things growing – reaching and spreading high and wide.

Finally, Eve appeared.

'What took you so long?' Scott asked.

'Couldn't find it,' she said, holding up her revolver.

It was a lie, but he didn't want to call her on it. 'Are you ready?'

She nodded, still scanning all around. 'Let's go.' She got into the driver's seat, started the engine and pulled away.

The roads through Wales and Snowdonia, as on the way in, were narrow and windy, but clear. Being on the more substantial roads from Manchester to Liverpool made him feel they were increasingly conspicuous and therefore in more danger. There were only three places where they had to slow down and manoeuvre carefully between barricades of self-driving cars. When they got close to the centre of Liverpool, Scott pulled over next to a tall building that appeared to have been, at one time, offices.

'We should take our time,' he said. 'I'll go to the top and look around. Do you have the binoculars?'

Eve reached over to the back seat and pulled out a pair.

'You wait here,' he said. Her fear of heights had worsened as she'd got older. 'We'll use the walkie-talkies to stay in touch.'

Eve took out two solid-looking walkie-talkies from a rucksack. She tested them, turning dials and pressing buttons.

'I'll look,' he said, and opened the door. Then he noticed a movement in the back of the 4×4. Grabbing his revolver, he pointed it at the tarpaulin that was covering whatever was moving.

'Stop!' he said to the covering, then motioning for Eve to train her gun on it too.

'Wait!' a voice said from beneath.

'Gavin?' Eve said.

Scott pulled at the plastic sheet. 'What are you doing here? I told you to stay with the others.'

Gavin smiled back at them. 'I couldn't leave you to come alone. It's too dangerous.'

What Gavin thought he might contribute wasn't obvious, and the look Eve gave Scott conveyed the same thought.

Gavin stood, pushing back the tarpaulin and reaching for his rucksack. 'You could walk into anything.'

Scott couldn't work out if he wanted Gavin to have brought the AI with him or not. But the way he swung the rucksack onto his back made him suspect he hadn't.

Gavin jumped out of the 4×4 and onto the ground beside Scott. 'I left it there,' he whispered. 'Hidden.'

Scott nodded and checked Eve hadn't heard him.

'I couldn't stay behind,' he said again.

'You're here now,' Scott said. 'And we can't go back.'

Gavin was clearly relieved and reached in his pocket to show Scott his revolver.

Scott lifted his walkie-talkie to show Eve. 'I'll stay in touch.'

Eve nodded. Scott recognised her fierce defiance – her desire to go with him to prove she wasn't afraid.

'I need you stay here,' Scott added, hoping to take the choice away from her.

Reluctantly, she nodded.

Scott left Eve at the entrance to the building and led Gavin inside, edging through the smashed glass frontage. They took the stairs, Gavin leading the way, eager.

It took over ten minutes to reach the top floor. Scott had to force open a door into the office space. There were no bodies, only several desks and meeting rooms, all caked in dust. On the tables were the usual things: photographs of families and loved ones, brimming in- and out-trays, holo-screen units, mugs, pens. There appeared to be the possibility of humanity returning at any moment.

Gavin led the way to the windows at the far end and looked out over Liverpool. Scott followed. The docks and sea stretched from one side of the window to the other, and beyond. He'd not been to the coast for over two years, and as he watched the slow-moving grey sea and even greyer clouds, he felt the desire to stand on the beach and wait for the waves come towards him, breaking one after the other.

He took his time scanning the surrounding area through binoculars, his movements tiny and specific.

'What do you think?' Gavin asked him.

'I don't see anyone,' he said. 'And there are lots of places to spring a trap.'

He felt Gavin move closer.

Scott shifted the binoculars towards the docks. Two huge ships leaned against one another, having collided, both prows battered and scarred, half submerged. Again Scott recalled how everything had stopped on the night of the Rapture. Looking at the two colossal ships, he wondered how humans had managed it – how they'd figured such huge hunks of metal could ever float.

'Nobody,' he said. 'Not in this direction, anyway.'

'We need to take a closer look,' Gavin said, already heading for the stairs.

'I don't like it,' Scott said.

'You always say that.'

'You're used to seeing cities this way,' Scott said. 'I'm not.'

It was true. Gavin and Eve were babies when the Rapture happened. They'd grown up in this world, empty of people. It was different for Scott; he saw the world like a ghost land. He remembered what it had been like: cities like Liverpool teemed with life, were always on the move, always noisy, and always changing. There was no getting used to the quiet or the stillness of cities as they were now. Their size and complexity felt incongruous with their inactivity. Cities were there because of people – they had risen higher and higher to house people because there was not enough space on the ground. Now there was all the space in the world.

'Let's go,' Scott said, and followed Gavin to the stairs where he activated the walkie-talkie. 'We're on our way down,' he told Eve.

THIRTEEN

SCOTT PEERED through the gaps in the towering edifices, over to the Royal Liver Building in the distance, keeping it on his right. He led the way, Eve and Gavin following in single file, moving as silently as they could. Memories of visiting Liverpool years before came to him but were sparse and inaccurate. Thankfully, the city was clustered around the docks and the sea, so he followed the landscape downwards to the west, hoping to find signs of survivors. He knew how difficult they would be to discover; it was the only way of staying hidden from the Watchers.

The squawking of seagulls made Scott look up. So many buildings, all of them devoid of life. The Albert Dock was up ahead and he looked over his shoulder to check the others were close by. He couldn't imagine anyone else there, still alive; the city was too massive, too still, to be home to anyone.

Sticking to the narrowest streets, Scott led the way to the docks and a row of buildings supported with red columns. He'd visited the Liverpool Tate art gallery with Rebecca many years before. Maybe the works of art were still in

THE VIOLET DAWN

there. He recalled there being a huge Jackson Pollock running along one wall. All that priceless artwork – and now 'priceless' meant something different.

'Why here?' Eve whispered.

Scott didn't know. All he had to go on was his own instinct – this was where he would stay if he wanted to hide in Liverpool. Being close to the sea appealed to him.

Scott stopped near a door into a building beside the docks.

'They could be anywhere,' he whispered to Eve. 'Being here makes you realise how difficult it is to find a small group of people in a city this size.'

'Hopefully they'll see us,' Eve said, edging out into the open, looking towards the sea, then back at the city centre.

'Don't stand out in the open, you—'

'Wait!' she said, appearing to sniff the air.

'What?' Gavin asked.

'Don't move,' Eve said, holding up one hand.

'What is it?' Scott whispered.

'Not sure.' Eve's eyes narrowed, focussing on something in the distance. 'I think there's someone down by the docks.'

Scott wanted to look himself but knew it was better to let Eve call the shots.

In a flash, Eve was running. Gavin was close behind her. Scott checked his revolver and followed.

Eve was already out of view by the time Scott had reached full speed, so he had to follow Gavin, who was also almost out of sight. Scott ran, his lungs and legs burning already. He weaved in and out of alleyways and ended up crossing a wide road filled with self-drivers, meaning he was more out in the open than he wanted to be. He tried to find cover, but there was none. With no other choice, he stopped running and listened for signs of either Eve or Gavin. All he heard was his own heavy breathing. He tasted metal on his tongue. The sound of shouting made him spin and head off again. He ran alongside the docks and took a right into a square surrounded by abandoned restaurants and bars. There was Eve, holding a small girl who was trying to kick and squirm her way out of Eve's grasp. Gavin reached them and helped hold the girl, who screamed in frustration.

Scott checked for signs of someone else, not thinking a young girl would be out on her own. He pushed his revolver into his coat pocket. They were in the centre of a square surrounded by buildings – easy pickings for Watchers planning on trapping them.

'She can't be out on her own,' Scott said, panting.

Gavin pointed his revolver at different parts of the buildings surrounding them. The girl had given up and was gasping noisily in Eve's arms, tears streaming down her face, a quiet anger simmering.

Scott got down on his knees. 'We won't hurt you,' he said to the girl. 'We're here to help.'

'We need to find cover,' Eve said, releasing her grip on the girl and resting her hands on the girl's shoulders.

Scott nodded and, still on his knees, peered up at the buildings surrounding the square.

'There,' Eve said, pointing.

Scott followed her finger to a broken glass door.

'Let's go,' Scott said.

The girl screamed and again kicked out at Eve, breaking free. 'I'm not going in there!'

Gavin caught hold of the girl's waist, lifting her off the ground.

'Be careful,' Scott said. 'Don't hurt her.' He took her from Gavin and placed her on her feet. 'It's okay,' he told her.

'Really. We're not going to hurt you. But there are people who might want to hurt all of us, so we need to hide.'

The girl's forehead creased with anger, and she pressed her lips together so hard they were white.

'Where can we hide?' Scott asked her.

The girl relaxed and her lips opened.

'Come on, kid,' Gavin said.

'Don't,' Scott said, glancing at Gavin. He let go of the girl's arms. 'I promise. We want to help you.'

The girl shook her head.

Scott stared at the broken glass door the girl had refused to walk through. 'What's in there?'

The girl glanced at the door, then shook her head.

'We need to go,' Eve said to Scott. 'We can't stay out in the open.'

Scott ignored her.

'We don't have to go in there,' Scott said to the girl. 'You tell us where we should go.'

'Is this a good idea?' Gavin asked.

Again, Scott ignored the suggestion and looked the girl in the eyes. He waited.

Finally, the girl turned and walked the opposite way – towards a restaurant on the opposite side of the square. Scott followed and motioned for Eve and Gavin to do the same.

FOURTEEN

THE GIRL LED Scott into what had once been an Italian restaurant. Many of the tables were still dressed with tablecloths, pepper and salt grinders, and folded napkins. Others had been cleared out of the way so there was a walkway to the kitchen at the far end of the building. The girl led them through the restaurant, pushed through the kitchen doors, and continued to a set of stairs. She stopped at the bottom, appearing to listen for something or someone.

'What is it?' Scott whispered.

The girl ignored him and began to climb the stairs. Scott watched her, glanced back at Eve, then climbed them himself.

The girl held open the door for him at the top. Her expression was uncertain.

'In here?' Scott asked.

The girl nodded and walked further into the dark room.

Scott held his breath, his heart pounding, then walked through the door. He peered into the room and saw a figure on a mattress in the far corner. It was a woman, her hair long, spread over the sheets she had pulled up high against her chest. Hesitantly, Scott walked over to her.

'My name's Scott.'

The woman opened her eyes and tried to speak, but only managed a gasp before closing her eyes once again. She appeared unwell, was covered in dirt and what he guessed was dried blood smeared across her nose and mouth.

'Is this your daughter?' Scott asked, glancing over at the girl, who stood watching.

The woman nodded. Her eyes were dark, her lips cracked, her skin sallow. Something about the smell in the room told Scott she would not last much longer. He felt for the child, who had clearly been looking after her mother for some time.

'Here,' Eve said, handing Scott a bottle of water. The girl took the bottle from Scott before dropping to her knees and helping her mother drink.

'Where are the others?' Gavin asked.

The woman swallowed the water with some effort, grimacing. With the girl's help, she sat up, using the wall behind to support her head.

'Will you help her?' the woman asked, her voice husky, barely audible.

He couldn't promise anything, so he changed the subject. 'Are there others?' he asked.

The woman closed her eyes, wincing with pain, and shook her head. 'Gone.'

'They've left Liverpool?'

The woman opened her eyes and looked at her daughter. 'Someone ... something killed them. Most of them.'

Scott sat back on his heels and felt his stomach sink. 'Most?'

'Except River,' the woman said, pointing at her daughter before coughing. 'And two other men. They left on a boat.' She kissed River on her forehead. 'You won't find the men. I don't know where they were going.'

'How did you survive?'

'I wasn't here when he ... it ... came.'

'It? What do you mean? Who killed them? A Watcher?'

The woman glanced again at the girl. 'I don't like to talk about it. While...' She nodded at the girl.

Scott placed a hand on the woman's arm. 'What can we do to help?'

'Take her with you.'

The young girl held on to her mother's arm more tightly.

'We can't,' Eve said, edging closer.

Scott gave her a stern look.

'It's a trap,' Eve said. 'Think about it. Only one girl left... We'd have to take her, and they know that. They're waiting for us to do this.'

'You have to,' the woman said, desperate. 'I can't hang on much longer. I don't know what's wrong with me, but I know there's no stopping it.'

It did appear suspicious, but the way Eve was going about it was thoughtless – all wrong.

'We'll take her,' Gavin said, staring at Eve. 'We can't leave her here.'

'But Eve's right,' Scott said reluctantly. 'It looks like a trap.'

'We'll make sure no one's following us,' Gavin said. 'What's the alternative? We just leave her here?'

'Please,' the woman said.

'We can take you both somewhere safe,' Scott said. 'Find a surgical-machine.'

'No,' the woman said. 'It's no use. Please. Take River with you. Look after her.'

Gavin offered the girl his hand; she retreated and held on to her mother.

The woman said the girl's name sharply; it looked to have taken all her strength. 'River. Stop. I need you to do as Mummy says.'

The girl cried silently, now and then wiping her eyes with the back of her hand. 'No, Mummy. I want to stay with you.'

'Listen to me,' her mother said. 'I'm dying, and you need someone to look after you.'

The woman's honesty and the word 'dying' struck Scott hard. To tell her daughter must have been the worst thing she'd ever had to say, yet she'd said it so freely. The only way to make the girl listen was to be honest. She'd spoken the truth, and even at such a young age the girl knew it. It would have been easy for the woman to pretend, to tell her daughter a story about following her once she was better. But she didn't do that.

Scott looked at Eve and gave her a look of capitulation. There was no way they could leave the girl with her dying mother.

The girl wrapped her arms around her mother's neck, kissing her. Already the woman appeared weaker.

Gavin reached for her again, but this time the girl didn't fight. Picking her up so her head rested on his shoulder, Gavin carried her out of the room and down the stairs, followed by Eve.

'Don't go in there,' the woman said weakly.

Scott didn't understand, and took his time to work out what she meant rather than asking her to speak again. He recalled the building the girl didn't want them to enter.

'River,' the woman said, 'she saw it happen. She said the man had strange eyes.'

'What do you mean, strange?'

The woman coughed. 'She said they shone in the darkness – they were purple.'

Scott froze.

'What does it mean?' the woman asked. 'It killed all of them with a revolver. Those who survived, like River and the two men, must have been saved by the empty chamber. It did it like the Watchers – but it wasn't a Watcher.'

The woman's eyes filled with tears of horror. 'Can you imagine? Waiting for it to happen...' She winced and leaned back against the wall. Scott helped her lie down so she was more comfortable.

'Go,' the woman said. 'Before they come back.'

Scott stood. 'Can I ... do anything?'

The woman lowered her gaze to his pocket and his revolver. A single tear ran down her cheek and onto the mattress.

'We'll look after her,' Scott said. He took the revolver from his pocket and placed it on the mattress beside her.

The woman closed her eyes. 'Thank you.'

Scott left the room, descended the stairs and exited the building into the early evening. Eve, Gavin and the girl were outside the door, hidden beneath a porch roof.

Across the square was the glass door through which the girl had refused to enter. He knew what he'd find there, but he had to look inside.

'Wait here,' he said to Eve and Gavin. 'I won't be long.'

'Is that a good idea?' Eve asked, the young girl in her arms.

Scott didn't answer, only pursed his lips before heading across the square. He stepped through the broken window, his feet crunching on the shards of glass. Maybe there were other survivors. The hope faded when, after climbing to the first floor, he recognised the stench of dead bodies. He wasn't used to it; the dead after the Rapture didn't decompose in the same way. He stopped on the stairs, gripping the banister. His legs shook, his heart raced, and a cold sweat spread across his back. It wasn't worth seeing the bodies; there was nothing to gain from it. Better to turn back. But his feet took two more steps and he was climbing again. Reaching the top floor, he entered the room, trying not to predict what he might see, but accept whatever was there. It was important that he acknowledged the dead – they deserved that. The room was dark. Scott took the torch from his rucksack and pointed it at the ceiling, not wanting to reveal what had now crept into his thoughts. Slowly, he lowered the torch.

One, two, three bodies laid out on the floor in a row.

Ten, eleven, twelve...

They lay motionless.

He should burn the place to the ground. Those words he knew would have been spoken before shooting each one of them. He imagined what it must have been like for River, hearing the guns go off, maybe seeing each person fall forward. Then a revolver pushed against the back of her own head, followed by the empty click. Scott rolled his hand into a fist, and his arm shook. Burn it to the ground – all of it. He would return and burn it all.

As he was about to leave, his torch swept across the back wall, revealing something written in large lettering. Black paint dripped from each letter. He scanned the graffiti: THE VIOLET DAWN IS RISING.

Scott couldn't move the beam away from the words.

FIFTEEN

EVE HELD ON TO RIVER, waiting for Scott to return. She knew what was in there – and knew Scott would lie about it. Being here, she knew it was what she'd seen in the vision she'd had when she held the black box. And it was someone like her who had done it. She knew that now. And what scared her most was seeing the same ability in herself. It was dark and distant, but still, when she looked inward, she saw her ability to do such a thing. It was cold, calculating, machine-like. Yes, that's what it was – machine-like.

She stood River beside her and held her hand. 'It'll be okay,' Eve told her.

'You're safe now,' Gavin said.

It sounded ridiculous coming from Gavin, because there was nothing he could do to help her even if he wanted to. Gavin was more of a hindrance than a help. Not that she could ever tell him so.

Eve felt River turning the gold ring on her middle finger. It was the ring Scott had given her from the tooth fairy all those years ago. She had always worn it, yet never gave it much thought.

THE VIOLET DAWN

'Do you like rings?' she asked River.

River's attention was drawn from the door Scott had disappeared into. The girl knew what was up there too.

'Rings?' Eve said again. 'You like them, huh?'

River stared at the ring on Eve's finger and touched it gently.

'Want to try it on?' Eve asked her.

River shook her head.

'It's okay,' Eve said. 'Go ahead, try it.' She took off the ring and offered it to the little girl.

River reached out hesitantly for it, before pushing it onto her own middle finger.

'It'll slip off that finger,' Eve said. 'I used to wear it on my thumb.' She swapped the ring to River's thumb. 'Perfect.'

River stared at the ring, turning her hand one way then the other.

Gavin nudged Eve as Scott emerged from the building.

'What was up there?' Gavin asked.

Scott shook his head and swallowed. 'Nothing.'

Lies, she thought. All Scott ever did was tell lies.

'What was it?' she asked, her voice stern.

Scott smiled at River.

'I know what's in there,' Eve said.

'What do you mean?' Scott asked.

'I know,' she said.

Scott took a deep breath. 'Then you know why I'm not saying it.' He glanced at River.

'She was there,' Eve said. 'Remember?'

'What do you want from me?' Scott snapped. 'Let's go. There's nothing left for us here.'

Holding River's hand, Eve followed Scott, looking up at the building he had been in. The black box had wanted to show her what was up there – the bodies, the four others with violet eyes. The AI in the black box wanted to communicate with her, but she didn't understand how that was possible … or what the AI wanted.

They walked purposefully through Liverpool, no longer hiding. Eve knew, like Scott, that taking River with them was a bad idea. Whoever it had been with the violet eyes, if they wanted to set a trap, the little girl was the perfect way to do it. When they took her back to the others, it would show whoever was waiting the way. But they couldn't leave the young girl alone there with her dead mother.

When they reached the 4×4, Eve got into the passenger seat and Gavin sat in the back with River. Scott glanced across at her, but she ignored him. Now was not the time. In fact, she wasn't sure the time would ever come for him to be honest with her.

SIXTEEN

SCOTT COULDN'T TELL them what he'd seen. On the way back to north Wales, it was some time before anyone spoke.

'What will we tell everyone?' Eve asked.

River was asleep on the back seat, her head resting on Gavin's lap, who stroked her hair away from her face.

'That everyone's dead,' Scott said. 'That's all they need to know.'

Eve sighed.

They sat in silence for two more miles.

'She's brave,' Gavin said, looking down at the sleeping girl. 'To leave her mother behind like that.'

'She had no choice,' Scott said. 'I think she knew that. Even at her age.'

'What do we do now?' Gavin asked. 'There are more Watchers every day, and fewer of us. I don't understand how Mathew convinces young people to become Watchers, even when they're not even old enough to remember the Rapture.'

'The only thing we can do is keep hiding,' Scott said.

'Like they did in Liverpool?' Eve said bitterly.

Scott recognised an impatience in her voice. He'd noticed it more and more over the past year. He waited, considering how best to respond.

'I think we should stop running,' Eve said.

Scott felt Gavin staring at him, waiting for his response.

'What do you suggest we do exactly?' Scott asked.

Eve was looking out of the window at the darkness. 'We find Mathew. End it before he finds any more survivors.'

There was no doubt in the way she spoke, even if it was a foolish idea. Not only were they outnumbered, but they were outgunned; Mathew had far more resources as far as weapons and ammunition went. Scott thought about the black box and the AI he had to keep out of Mathew's hands. It would be crazy to go headfirst into a mindless attack just because they were tired of running or hiding.

'How do we stop Mathew?' Scott asked Eve.

'I can stop him,' she said. 'Get me close enough and I'll stop him.'

Scott noticed her eyes shimmer violet. In her stare was the belief that she could do it – and part of Scott believed her. But there was so much she didn't know, or understand. He could tell her everything and see if any of it would change her mind. But it wouldn't – he knew that.

Scott focused on the road ahead, barely illuminated by the 4×4's side-lights, and thought through their choices. When had they started looking to him to make the final decisions? When he first found them, when Eve was a baby, there were so many of them. He'd been relieved. He'd added someone to their small group with River – something no one had done for several years. Yet their numbers were only going one way – down. There was no stopping it. Hiding from Mathew meant they could survive. But for how long? What was he waiting for? Maybe it was Eve he was waiting

THE VIOLET DAWN

for – to grow older and take over, help make the decisions that would lead to their survival. Then the image of a man with eyes the same as Eve's came to his mind. He'd been told there were others.

He drove on autopilot. Before long he recognised the silhouette of the Welsh mountains in the distance. He weaved along the narrow roads, now and then having to go off-road to avoid self-drivers parked in the road or trees that had fallen and obstructed their way through.

Finally, he turned in to the lodge, stopped and turned off the engine. They'd done a good job of making the buildings appear empty. From where he was, he almost doubted there was anyone living there. On the back seat, River had woken and was looking through the window. She rubbed her eyes and Scott saw the instant she recalled what had happened.

Scott opened the door for the young girl, who shuffled along the back seat and out into the cold air. He walked her to the lodge and saw a dark figure appear in the doorway. It was Elidi, her arms wrapped around herself.

'Who do we have here?' Elidi asked River in a soft voice.

'This is River,' Scott said. 'She's come to stay with us.'

Elidi covered her mouth with a hand, her eyes filling with tears. Scott thought it was amazing how Elidi read situations, how she registered another's mood or emotion within moments. It took no explaining.

'Sweetheart,' Elidi said to River, smiling, her voice warm. 'You must be cold, hungry and tired. No little girl should be any of those things, never mind all three.'

The girl looked back at Eve, who stood beside Scott, then back up to Elidi. The girl nodded and took Elidi's hand.

'Thank you,' Scott said to Elidi. He was also tired and needed to lie down.

Gavin walked past Scott and Eve into the building, not

stopping to speak. Eve threw her bag into a corner inside the building and made for the kitchen.

Scott walked through the reception area and along the corridor to his room, where he undressed and got beneath the covers. It was early morning: sunrise was hours away. He closed his eyes and saw all the bodies in Liverpool, in a line, lying where they'd been shot. There was a callous disregard for their bodies – as though they were unimportant. But their souls had made it to Heaven, and that's all that mattered. He wanted to go back, take the bodies, one at a time, and burn them in the square. He vowed again that when it was all over he'd burn the place down.

He felt cold when he thought about River's mother. She wouldn't live long – she had been waiting for Scott to get there. It was a strange thought, but one that made perfect sense; she'd held on for as long as necessary. Now there was someone to look after River, she could let go. He rolled onto his back and stared at the ceiling. He heard Elidi and River walk past his room. There was a warmth about Elidi that he saw as purely feminine. He remembered Freya and how she spoke to him in the dead of night – how she'd asked if he was okay, asked why he couldn't sleep, or whether he'd dreamed of her. Elidi's door closed softly. The only sound was the wind in the trees, their branches tapping against the glass.

He recalled the graffiti on the wall, the paint dripping, then he saw two violet eyes peering back at him through the darkness.

SEVENTEEN

SHE TOOK SOME CONVINCING, but Scott coaxed Eve outside to sit with him beneath the oak tree in the park. It was rare for them to sit out in the open, but they hadn't seen any sign of Watchers for months and it was so beautiful outside, Scott wanted to make the most of the warmth. At times like this, Scott felt as though he was showing Eve things that meant a lot to him. The simple idea of a bright summer's day, being outside beneath the shade of a tree, was important to him in a way he hadn't considered before. More and more, he realised that the things he'd always taken for granted were important, even essential. They were part of what it meant to be alive.

Eve had taken to studying mathematics and physics. Within days, the books, theorems and ideas she was learning were beyond Scott's comprehension. Since she was only eight, he thought he should hide this from others, but they'd grown accustomed to her precociousness as much as he had, and thought nothing of it. Or at least, they hid their suspicions well enough.

With books scattered around her chair, she scribbled numbers, symbols and graphs on paper, now and then stopping to reach for another book.

'What are you doing exactly?' he asked.

Eve sighed and put down her pen. 'In these books, I have found several mathematical problems that no one could solve until we created the AI. But it doesn't tell me how they were solved.'

When Scott had described the AI to her, she had been fascinated by the idea and spent hours researching the concept.

'The mathematical problems?'

'Like the Riemann hypothesis,' she said. *'It concerns the distribution of prime numbers. It says in this book that it remained unsolved for nearly two hundred years before the AI discovered the answers.'*

'And you want to work it out yourself?'

Eve appeared hurt for a moment, then shrugged.

Scott nodded, unsure what to say.

Eve closed the book on her lap and reached down to the grass for another, but yelped in pain and jerked back into her chair.

Scott was out of his seat in an instant. *'What?'*

Her arms and hands moved quickly, her body stiffening. She stood, her hands rolled into fists, her brow furrowed, her mouth fixed.

'What is it?' Scott asked.

She closed and then opened her eyes. They were a deep violet, deeper than they'd ever been before. She stared straight ahead.

Scott held her arm. She pushed him away and he fell to the ground. She was strong and didn't hold back. She continued to stare straight ahead.

'What is it?' he asked again, standing.

Slowly, she unfurled her fist and held her hand out in front of her, cupped, holding something. Scott stared at her hand; she was holding a dead wasp. With her other hand, she rubbed her leg where the wasp had stung her. She'd caught it. Her eyes darkened further, a purple-violet swirl pulsing in and out. Lifting her hand *to her face, she examined the wasp, crushed, its body flickering in the warm breeze. She let it go, dropping it to the ground.*

'Are you okay?' Scott asked, wary of getting close again.

She flinched as though only just becoming aware he was there and, like someone sleepwalking, she stared straight through him.

She shook her head, and her eyes were brown again. She stumbled and Scott reacted quickly, stopping her from falling. She started to cry.

'My hand,' she said.

It was covered in stings.

Scott took her into the house they'd been using at the edge of the park and dipped her hand in cold water. He recalled his mother, when he was Eve's age and had been stung by a bee, dousing his arm in vinegar. He could smell it, the way it made the back of his throat tingle. He looked through the cupboard and found a bottle of vinegar, years old by now, opened the lid and sniffed it. He recognised the smell, but it was accompanied by something else – musty and sour. Deciding not to use it, he went out to the bus to search through the supply of medicine they carried with them. He found antiseptic and painkillers. It was all he could do to help.

When he returned, Eve still had her hand submerged in the water.

'What happened?' she asked. 'I remember reaching for a book and then everything went black.'

'You don't remember?'

She shook her head. 'The next thing I remember is being here with my hand ... my hand in this water.'

It had happened before, but not for so long or so intensely. When she was anxious, or in pain, or felt threatened, her eyes turned violet and something inside her took over. He'd tried to ignore this happening in the past, but there was no way he could this time. What Mathew and Samuel had told him was true – and he didn't know what to do.

Eve cried quietly. 'What's happening to me?'

Scott didn't know what to say. He handed her two pills and a bottle of water. 'Take these.'

'I don't want to,' she said.

'It will help with the pain.'

She shook her head slowly then frowned, as if remembering something.

'What?' Scott asked.

She took her hand from the water and wiped it against her T-shirt. 'The mathematics problem. I know how the AI did it.'

Scott didn't like it when she mentioned the AI. Whenever she did, it reminded him she had no idea of the truth.

'The maths problem?'

She nodded and ran out to the park for her books. She dropped to her knees and flicked through one of them until she found the page she was looking for. With fierce movements, she scribbled in her notebook, now and then looking back to the textbook, reading, then returning to her own notes.

He would have to tell her soon. But it never took long for Eve to return to the girl she always was. The violet eyes and cold stare disappeared, and he'd question his own eyes and what he thought he might have seen. He sat on his chair again, reached for his book and opened it.

Eve sat back on her heels and covered her mouth. He saw she'd worked it out.

He tried to read, but it was impossible.

EIGHTEEN

SCOTT WAS WOKEN ABRUPTLY, everything moving violently and without warning. He opened his eyes, but it was dark. He reached for whatever was covering his head, then kicked out. 'Stop!'

No response. He stumbled and fell against a wall. More hands at his arms, pulling and tugging. There was someone else behind, pushing him. He lost his balance and fell. Someone lifted him up.

'What's going on?'

Another push in his back made him collide with a door that swung open, making him stumble and fall again. Two sets of hands pulled him up.

'Eve?' he shouted.

Still no response.

He was outside and the wind and rain took away his breath. They pushed him to his knees, his hand slipping in the wet grass. His body was lifted off the ground as someone kicked him in the stomach. He choked, unable to breathe. Lying on the ground, he tried to fill his lungs with air, telling himself to stay calm, that the air would return, but still he writhed, suffocating.

There was screaming and shouting, then a gunshot. Then even more desperate screaming and shouting.

He still couldn't breathe. His stomach and chest tightened, strangling his throat.

Another gunshot. A boot struck the base of his spine. Scott tried to crawl away from where the kick had come from. The desire to fight back made him attempt to get to his feet, but with only one hand, and with someone pushing him, it was impossible to maintain his balance. He crashed onto his side and landed on something hard.

Finally, he gasped and swallowed air.

'No!' he shouted. 'Stop!'

But this time a fist knocked his jaw sideways and he couldn't hear, couldn't work out which direction the fist had come from. On the ground, he clawed at the hood covering his head, but the more he tore at it, the more tightly it gripped his throat.

He heard Elidi protesting – demanding they stop. Then there was another deep thudding, and her voice disappeared.

Scott lay doubled over on the ground, curled up in a ball, an arm holding his stomach. If only he could breathe, regain his balance, take off the hood, he could fight back.

Another gunshot. He recognised the sound. It was a revolver – a Watcher's revolver.

'It has been a long time,' a voice said.

Scott waited, hoping there had been some mistake, hoping it was all a cruel joke.

'I told you I'd find you,' the voice said. 'Maybe I didn't think it would take this long, but still.'

'Mathew?' Scott said, his voice barely audible.

'A little older than when we last met, but yes, I'm still Mathew.'

'What are you doing?' Scott asked.

'What am I doing? What am I doing? Redeeming the whole of humanity. That small feat. Remember?'

'You're as insane as ever, I hear,' Scott said as he got to his feet, clutching his stomach and coughing.

'No,' Mathew said. Scott turned to see who Mathew was commanding, but the cloth hood permitted no light. 'Wait. There'll be time for that.'

'What happened to the meek and modest Watcher?' Scott asked.

'Times have changed. We have a job to do, and I'm afraid it has proven more difficult than I had initially considered. But we are nearly there.'

'How many are left?' Scott asked.

'In the world? Less than four thousand. All here in Britain.'

Scott heard a revolver being opened and its chamber spun.

'How can you be sure?' Scott asked.

'We have developed reliable tracking equipment.'

'You mean the AI?' Scott asked.

'Not so intricate,' Mathew said. 'But effective all the same. We knew you'd find the girl eventually, and bring her back with you. It was simply a matter of time.'

Beneath the hood, Scott closed his eyes and waited.

Hands worked at the hood, and with a swipe someone snatched it away. Bright lights in the darkness blinded him. He covered his eyes then blinked through the rain. He scanned the people outside for Eve, but couldn't see her.

Mathew appeared in front of him. 'You have done well to keep them hidden for so long.'

'Please,' Scott said. 'Don't hurt them.'

'Well,' Mathew said, 'that will be your decision to make.'

Scott rubbed his eyes. He could just make out a row of people on their knees. Women and children, all of them tied up, blindfolded and gagged.

Scott tried to get up. 'What are you doing?' he shouted. 'You can't. They've done nothing wrong.'

They beat him down again.

'Nothing wrong?' Mathew said, turning to them. 'They are all sinners, Scott. You know this.'

Scott searched frantically for Eve. There was no sign of her or Gavin.

'There are children here. You can't do this!'

Mathew looked concerned for a moment, his eyes focusing on the small figure of River next to Elidi and Daker.

'I don't want it to be this way,' Mathew said. 'And you can end it quickly.'

'What do you want?'

'What I want is to give these people what *they* want.'

'What they want? Ask them,' Scott said. 'Ask them if they want you to kill them.'

'It doesn't work like that. They are God's children. And, like children, they need guidance. We must do what we know is right, whether or not they see it.'

'Please, Mathew. I'm begging you. Don't do this.' Scott knew what would happen – he'd seen the aftermath of the same thing in Liverpool.

'Where's the AI?' Mathew asked. 'Give me the AI and you can buy them some time.'

Scott stared at the ground. 'I destroyed it.'

Mathew nodded to the Watcher, who took out his revolver and aimed it at Harriet, a young woman at the end of the row. Muffled screams and crying came from the women and children.

'Wait!' Scott said.

Mathew shook his head, both in disbelief and defiance. 'Where is it?'

'It's gone. I destroyed it years ago.'

Mathew took a deep breath, then turned to look along the line. He walked to the middle of the row, to where Elidi knelt, blindfolded. She straightened her back and lifted her head towards Mathew, who had taken his revolver from the pocket of his long coat. He glanced back at Scott.

'Please,' Scott said. 'I don't have it. If I did, I would give it to you.'

Mathew opened the cylinder on his revolver. He checked there was an empty chamber and spun it before closing it with a click.

Mathew lifted the revolver and pointed it at Elidi's head. He leaned towards her, the end of the revolver touching Elidi's forehead. He took a deep breath and said, 'The Watcher's revolver has five bullets and one empty chamber. This empty chamber belongs to Him, to do wi—'

'Wait!' Scott said.

Elidi's shoulders slumped and she bowed her head. The women and children cried through their gags.

Mathew lowered his revolver and turned to Scott.

'Okay,' Scott said. 'Let them go and you can have it.'

Mathew put the revolver in his pocket and walked over to Scott. The rain pattered against the shoulders of Mathew's long grey coat. He stared at Scott, his mouth straight, his brow a straight line.

'Tell me,' he said. 'Tell me where it is.'

NINETEEN

A SHORT, muscular Watcher untied Scott and helped him stand. Looking along the line of hooded women and children, Scott still didn't see Gavin or Eve.

The sound of voices coming from one building made Mathew stop and turn. Scott followed his line of sight and peered through the darkness.

It was Eve.

Scott shivered in the night air, knowing what was about to happen; he saw it all mapped out before him, the next few minutes. He would lose Eve for good, and there was nothing he could do.

Mathew pushed the revolver into his coat pocket and opened his arms wide. 'Eve,' he said. 'You've grown into a beautiful young woman. Look at you!'

The Watcher behind Eve pushed her towards Mathew. With her arms tied behind her back, Eve fell against Mathew, who held her. She pushed against him until he released her.

'You're a monster,' she snarled.

'Where has the time gone?' Mathew asked. 'It's hard to believe.'

'You can't do this,' Eve said, facing the row of women and children, all tied and gagged. 'You can't!'

Mathew turned to look too. 'Soon they will be with Him. It's unfortunate, granted. I don't like this. It would have been better for the Rapture to have taken every soul. But the Lord works in mysterious ways.'

'You don't have to do this,' Scott said. 'Let them go.'

Mathew was no longer interested in Scott – he was staring at Eve, a wry smile curling his lips. 'She doesn't know,' he said. 'Does she?'

'I can get it,' Scott said. 'Please. Don't.'

Eve fought against the ties around her wrists.

Mathew, with raised chin, walked closer to her.

'No!' Scott said. 'Don't. Leave her alone.'

Mathew's eyes were fixed on Eve the whole time. He held her shoulders and motioned for her to turn around. She stared up at Mathew, breathing heavily.

'I will untie you,' Mathew said. 'Allow me.'

Eve glanced at Scott then back up at Mathew, who towered over her. She turned around and Mathew untied her. The rope fell to the ground. Eve flexed her shoulders and rubbed her wrists.

Mathew continued to stare at her. Then, quietly, narrowing his eyes, he spoke to her. 'You've seen them, haven't you?'

With her eyes fixed on Mathew, she backed away towards Scott.

'Seen who?' Scott asked.

Mathew and Eve ignored him. Mathew watched Eve, his eyes open wide with a willingness to read what was happening.

'Please,' Scott said. 'Let them go. I'll fetch the AI and you can have it.'

Mathew wiped the side of his nose with a finger, all the time looking from Eve to Scott and back again.

He spoke to Eve. 'You have, haven't you? You've seen them?'

'I know what you and the AI did,' she said.

Mathew nodded. 'You do?'

Scott didn't understand what they were talking about.

'They designed the AI to help humanity,' Eve said. 'Not bring about its end.'

'Is that so?'

'You misused its knowledge. And we will always remember you for doing so.'

'Who will remember me?'

'Humanity will survive.'

Mathew waited, a wry smile creeping across his face.

Eve took a step closer to Scott.

Mathew turned to Scott and rubbed his hands. 'How are we going to do this? She appears to know a lot less than I thought she might, for someone who has circled the sun eighteen times.'

Scott shook his head. 'Don't,' he said. He sensed Eve's eyes on him. He couldn't look at her.

'I'm surprised, Scott. Really. The whole holier-than-thou act you have going on doesn't extend to the one person it should.'

'What are you talking about?' Eve asked. 'Dad? What's he talking about?'

'Dad?' Mathew said laughing. 'This gets better and better.'

Scott tipped his head back, took a deep breath and

closed his eyes. There was no stopping what was about to happen.

'I will get the AI,' Scott said. 'It is here.' He pointed to the lodge. 'But don't do this. There's no benefit to you in doing it.'

'It is remarkable how a person's whole demeanour, their tone of voice, changes when it is in their interest to do so.' Mathew walked towards Eve, all the time talking to Scott. 'Where is the AI?'

'It's gone,' Eve said. 'Scott destroyed it eighteen years ago.'

Mathew shook his head slowly and smiled. 'Is that what he told you?' His eyes narrowed. 'But you know it's here, don't you?' He glanced at Scott. 'Do you want to tell her? This will be a lot easier if you confirm what I'm saying as we go.'

Scott looked at the ground. 'It's true,' he said to Eve and Mathew. 'I have the AI.'

It was clear Eve already knew this, and Scott felt foolish not having spoken to her about it. 'The AI left behind a version of its processing', he said, 'that would allow future programmers to bring it back to life.'

She didn't look as shocked as he thought she might.

'I should have told you,' he said. 'I was going to. But I didn't want to worry you. I didn't wa—'

'But why?' she asked. 'Why keep it at all? You know what it did. Why not destroy it?'

Scott rubbed his arms and recalled the tattooed hand he'd left behind in the hospital theatre all those years ago. Now all of that had been for nothing.

'He knows its importance,' Mathew said. 'He knows its worth. It would be like destroying the Sistine Chapel, the Mona Lisa. It would be an act of desecration.'

'I'll do it,' Eve said. 'In a heartbeat.'

Mathew smiled at her with a look of admiration. 'You would, wouldn't you? If you could.'

The rain had slowed, and behind the mountains the sky was growing lighter. It would soon be morning.

'You can stop me from talking,' Mathew said to Scott. 'And you can stop my Watchers from sending your friends to Him. For the time being, anyway. I know you don't think the same way as I do on this matter. All I want is the AI.'

Scott turned to the lodge. 'Give me five minutes. Alone. I'm not going anywhere.'

Mathew nodded. 'Five minutes. Then I won't be able to resist catching up with Eve. There's a lot we need to discuss.'

Scott stared at him and shook his head gently.

Mathew gestured for Scott to enter the lodge closest to them. 'Go ahead. We'll be waiting.'

Scott walked into the lodge, trying desperately to rack his brains for a way to change what was happening, and what would happen. But he saw no way out of it.

TWENTY

EVE WATCHED Scott enter the lodge.

'What?' she asked Mathew, who was staring at her.

'You can tell me what you saw,' Mathew said. 'You've seen them, haven't you?'

Eve knew he was talking about the four others with violet eyes she'd seen in her vision when she'd handled the black box.

'I am the only one who can help you,' he said. 'I have the answers you need. They saw you too.'

Eve ignored him, saw him move closer out of the corner of her eye.

'And Scott saw it, but not in the way you did. He was actually there – he saw all of them.'

'Who?' Eve asked.

'All of them. Saved. Each one of them. Except for three others. Including the girl.' Mathew pointed over to River, blindfolded and kneeling in the wet grass.

'You killed them all?' she asked.

'I freed them,' he said. 'I prefer to say freed.'

'I don't care what word you like to use for it. We both know what you did.'

Mathew nodded slowly. 'Tell me what you saw.'

Eve frowned then closed her eyes. She saw the four pairs of eyes looking back at her.

'Who are they?' she asked.

'I can tell you everything,' he said. 'Scott has kept it all from you. He believes he knows best.' Mathew glanced over to the lodge. 'Ask him,' he said. 'Ask him what he saw inside that building. You know and I know what was in there. But he will lie to you.'

'Why?' Eve asked. 'Why did you do that?'

'It's God's will. The empty chamber is His to do with as He wishes.'

'That makes no sense! You decided on the revolver with six bullets. You decide which chamber to leave empty. You choose how much to spin the cylinder. I know all about what you do – and it has nothing to do with God.'

'You saw their eyes, didn't you?'

'Who are they?'

'Ask Scott.'

'Stop!' she shouted. 'Just stop. Tell me.'

TWENTY-ONE

'GAVIN,' Scott said, 'it's me. I'm alone.'

He walked through the lodge, looking into the rooms as he passed them. Inside each one he saw the disturbance caused by Mathew and his Watchers. Bedclothes across the floor, overturned chairs and furniture, toys and dolls abandoned. He gritted his teeth and balled his hand into a fist.

'Gavin?' he said. 'I need you to come out.'

He walked into the last bedroom at the end of the corridor. No sign of him. Through the window, he could see the garden where Mathew and the Watchers had the women and children on their knees, lined up. The sun was rising, revealing colours: nightclothes, the Watchers' long grey coats he knew so well. Mathew was talking to Eve. There was no way he could keep the truth from her, yet even now, Scott wanted a way out, a way of explaining away the lies he'd kept up for so long. At first it hadn't been deliberate; it made sense for Eve to call him Dad. The box the AI had given him was hardly ever on his mind. It was there, like an old ornament, kept because of some vague sentimentality. But the biggest secret – that Eve was different in the most basic way – was always there, on his mind. It was there in the morning when he made her breakfast. It was there in the afternoon when he taught her to read and write. It was there in the evening when they played cards or when he read her stories. And it was there when he kissed her goodnight. This was the secret he knew Mathew would not keep to himself, whatever Scott did to try and prevent it.

'Gavin,' he said, louder this time, frustration in his voice.

Movement in one room made Scott walk out into the hallway. There was Gavin, his face and clothes dirty.

'I was beneath the floorboards,' he said, breathing heavily, pointing to the room next to him. 'I thought it was for the best. To keep it hidden.'

'You did the right thing.'

Gavin's shoulders relaxed, and he offered Scott the black box.

'That was brave,' Scott said, taking the AI.

Gavin leaned over to look out of the window. 'What's happening? What are they doing? I heard gunshots.'

'They're okay. For now.'

Gavin nodded. 'Is Eve okay?'

'Yes,' Scott said, turning the box in his hand.

'Mathew's come for the AI, hasn't he?'

Scott nodded. 'Among other things.'

Gavin appeared confused but before he could speak Scott said, 'We have little choice. I have to hand it over.'

'No,' Gavin said. 'You can't!'

'Either we hand it over or he kills them all and takes it anyway. Handing it over is the only way to keep everyone safe.'

'What makes you think he won't take the box and kill everyone?'

THE VIOLET DAWN

Scott raised the box. 'It's this he wants. And we don't have a choice.'

'Destroy it,' Gavin said, trying to take it back. 'Now. Let's destroy it.'

Scott held on to the box. 'We can't. We don't have a choice.'

'How many are there, outside?' Gavin asked. 'How many Watchers?'

Scott glanced at the window. 'Not sure. Six?'

Gavin turned around, looking for something. 'We'll get weapons. You and me, we—'

'It's no use.'

Gavin's face reddened.

'Stay here,' Scott said. 'Hide. If anything happens to me, at least you can escape.'

'No,' Gavin said. 'I want to come with you. I want to help.'

'You will be helping. If something happens to me, then I'll know there's still a chance you can retrieve the AI, or stop Mathew from using it.'

'We'll stop him together.'

Scott shook his head. 'I have to speak with him, give him the AI. We will have the chance to take it back. But I'll need you to help me do that. Stay here. Hide again.'

Gavin looked out of the window. 'But—'

'Gavin, please. Stay here. If anything happens to me, they'll need you.'

Outside, there were more muffled screams. He saw a Watcher holding a revolver to the back of Harriet's head.

'Time's up!' Mathew shouted.

Scott pointed to the room in which Gavin had hidden beneath the floorboards. 'I have to go. Hide!'

Gavin stared at him, then out of the window. Finally he

gave in. Scott followed him and watched Gavin move the last floorboard and slide into the space beneath the floor.

'Don't come out until there's complete silence.'

'But if there's the sound of gunfire again, I—'

'No,' Scott said. 'Not even then. You must stay hidden. If you come out, they'll kill you too. And there'll be no chance of stopping Mathew. Promise me.'

Tears of anger and frustration shimmered in Gavin's eyes. He nodded and pulled the last plank of wood across his face.

Scott stood and walked out of the lodge, the AI heavy in his hand.

TWENTY-TWO

SCOTT EMERGED from the building holding the black box.

'You have it?' Mathew said, unable to hide his eagerness to hold it.

Scott held the box to his chest and walked towards Mathew. 'Not yet,' he said, stopping. 'First, let them all go.'

Mathew turned to the Watchers and the women and children. He looked again at Scott and shook his head. 'You'll have to trust me. Let's face it, if I wanted to kill you and take the box, what could you do to stop me?'

'I'll destroy it. Here and now.'

Mathew smiled. 'You couldn't. The AI made that thing to withstand nuclear bombs. Look at it!'

Scott felt its weight: it was solid, an exact and precise object.

'Hand it over,' Mathew said.

'Don't,' Eve said. 'You can't let him have it.'

Scott glanced at the mountains in the distance. For a moment he saw himself running and hiding, taking the AI with him.

Mathew turned his head, then his shoulders, then his whole body, towards Eve.

'I have plenty of time,' he said to her, then turned to Scott. 'We've had a good chat, haven't we, Eve?'

Scott's jaw flexed.

'Your eyes,' Mathew said to Eve. 'Violet. They're stunning. More vibrant than any other eyes I've seen.'

Eve moved uncomfortably, glancing over at Scott.

'You saw what he'd written on the wall, Scott?' Mathew asked. 'You saw it?'

'Dad?' Eve said. 'What's he talking about?'

Scott gripped the black box.

'Well?' Mathew asked Scott. 'Dad? What did you see?'

Scott shook his head. 'I saw the evil you did to those innocent people.'

'Innocent?' Mathew spat. 'You know better than that. Now answer her. What was written on the wall?'

Scott's stomach sank and his throat tightened. 'The violet dawn is rising.'

Eve looked from Scott to Mathew and back again. 'What does that mean?'

'It means we have a lot to talk about,' Mathew said.

'Don't do this,' Scott said.

'What?' Eve asked, her forehead creased, her arms folded even more tightly across her chest.

Mathew walked closer to Eve. 'Let's begin ... well, at the beginning. Scott is not your father. But I think you've always known that. Deep down.'

Eve shook her head slowly. 'You're lying.'

Mathew turned to Scott. 'I think it's time, don't you?'

Scott focused on the black box in his hand. 'Eve, I've been a father to you all your life.'

THE VIOLET DAWN

'Now, that's cheating,' Mathew said. 'Although I'm sure it's true, that's not quite what I meant, is it?'

Scott grimaced. He wanted to go to her, hold her and explain – just the two of them. 'I'm not your biological father. But I am your father.'

Eve shook her head. 'You lied to me!'

'Not at first. It just happened that way. And I let you believe it. I—'

'Who is my real father?' Eve asked.

Mathew stared at her.

Eve registered his stare and staggered backwards. 'No!'

'Scott didn't lie about who your mother was. That's something, I guess. Your mother and I were in love.'

'He's lying,' Scott said.

'*I'm* lying?' Mathew said, smiling.

'No,' Eve said, her voice breaking.

'Enough of this,' Mathew said. 'Nicholas – take it.'

The Watcher with two different coloured eyes walked towards Scott, his revolver aimed at him. Scott was done, his will defeated. This was the Watcher who had killed Juliet. He stared at Mathew and didn't stop Nicholas taking the AI from him.

Mathew's whole body relaxed. He held out his hand to the Nicholas, who lowered his revolver and walked over to Mathew to hand it over. Mathew held it carefully. 'It's beautiful,' he said, more to himself than to anyone else. 'Quite beautiful.'

'Let them go,' Scott said. 'You gave your word.'

Mathew stared at the box.

'Let them go,' Scott repeated.

Mathew lifted his head and sighed. 'This is your father too,' he said, showing Eve the box.

'No!' Scott said, diving for Mathew, before being tackled to the ground by two Watchers.

Eve stared at the black box. 'I don't understand.'

'This,' Mathew said. 'Or, rather, a more sophisticated version. This is only the fundamental workings of its consciousness – the ingredients we need to bring it back to life. Incredible, isn't it?'

'Let me explain,' Scott said to Eve before one Watcher struck him across the face, blood spraying onto the wet grass.

'Stop!' Eve said, crying. 'Stop! Leave him alone!'

Scott's face burned, his jaw aching.

Mathew held out the black box to Eve to show her. 'Before Scott destroyed the AI, the AI created you. Eve, you're incredible. More incredible than you know.'

Eve shook her head. She tried to help Scott stand, but the Watcher held her back. 'Why? I don't understand.'

Scott spoke into the ground. 'I'm begging you...'

Mathew held the box in the air. 'We created the AI and the AI created you, Eve.'

The Watcher let go of Eve, who had given up struggling.

'Before Scott destroyed it, the AI developed a way of modifying the embryo your mother was carrying. You are far superior to any human.' Mathew lowered the box and again showed it to Eve. 'You're the best of us, left behind as a gift from a flawed humanity to the world – and maybe, in years to come, to the galaxy. You're special, Eve. You always have been and always will be.'

Eve fell backwards into the Watcher, thrashing her arms. She fell to the ground, her eyes fixed on the box.

Scott struggled to stand, his feet unable to find purchase on the muddy ground.

'You're lying,' Eve said. 'That makes no sense.'

'Scott?' Mathew said. 'There's no point hiding any of this now. You hate me for telling her. But truly, it's wrong to keep this from her.'

'I didn't know,' Scott said to Eve. 'Not for sure. I had no way of knowing for sure.'

'So you kept it from her?' Mathew said.

Scott looked at the ground, then up at the sky. He turned to Eve, who stared back at him, her eyes filled with anger.

'I only ever wanted the best for you,' he said. 'Believe me. I had no reason to believe what Mathew told me was true. I didn't tell you because I didn't want to believe it myself.'

'So it is true?' Eve asked.

Scott recalled all the times he'd considered it. The colour of her eyes, her intelligence, her precision, her clear thinking ... all of it. She was faster, stronger, more intelligent than anyone he'd ever known.

Scott nodded. 'It's true.'

TWENTY-THREE

IN NEWCASTLE, it was always cold and always wet. The houses they'd found were tucked away, hidden from view, but with a good enough view that the Watchers could not surprise them.

Scott watched Eve spoon soup from a bowl to her mouth. She'd grown into her two front teeth and the roundness of her face was slimming down into the same shape as her mother's. Her hair and eyes, mostly, were brown like Dawn's. He tried to find Mathew in her, but could never pinpoint his contribution. As in life, as in his paternal relationship to Eve, his presence was ephemeral. There were times when Scott had convinced himself what Mathew had told him was a lie.

Eve's spoon stopped. 'How did Mummy die?'

As her questions often did, this one caught him off-guard.

'Die?' Scott kept his eyes fixed on her spoon, which had begun to move again. He attempted not to look surprised by her question.

'Jenny says people knew the date they would die.'

Again, Scott tried not to react, but he needed a moment all the same. Hearing Eve say it brought it all back. Now, more than ever, the idea seemed frightening.

'Where did Jenny hear that?'

'She heard her mummy and daddy talking. Did Mummy know she would die?'

'Everyone knows they're going to die, sweetheart.'

'Not like that,' she said, dropping her spoon into her soup, rolling her eyes.

Scott waited. He wanted to tell her as much of the truth as he could. 'Yes. She knew the day she would die. Which is why there was nothing I could do.'

Eve's eyes flashed violet. For a moment Scott thought she was about to cry, but she didn't.

'You okay?' he asked her.

She nodded. 'It's just ... how did people know when they would die? Do you know when you will die?'

Scott couldn't help glancing at the end of his arm, where his hand should be. 'I thought I did. But it was wrong.'

'Wrong? Why wasn't Mummy's wrong?'

'I don't know. I wanted it to be wrong.'

Eve finished her soup. He was struck by how quickly she'd learned to use a spoon. She'd been eating soup in the same way, without spilling a drop, for years.

'Do you know when I will die?' she asked.

Scott leaned forward in his chair, resting his arms on the table. 'No.' It was a relief to tell her the truth without thinking about what he was telling her. But then came more truths that he could easily add to his answer. He could tell her she wouldn't grow old at all, that she would reach an optimum age and then stay the same. What child wouldn't want to hear they would live forever? But that would make her different, and he was sure no child wanted to hear that they were different.

Eve drank some water then stared at the glass. 'Am I going to die?'

Scott swallowed. Sometimes he felt she could read his mind. 'Yes,' he said.

'And go to Heaven?'

'Who told you about that?'

The stories continued. He hadn't told her about Heaven – had heard no one talk about it for years. It was as if the concept was innate.

'Jenny says that when you die you go to Heaven.'

'Did she? Do you believe her?'

Eve shrugged. 'Don't know. That's why I asked you.'

'I guess no one knows for sure.'

And like that, he was part of a story as old as civilisation. Talking to Eve often meant the truth was elusive, and he didn't know why exactly. It just was. No matter how many times he told himself he would tell her the truth, he couldn't bring himself to do so.

'But Mummy is in Heaven, isn't she?'

'If there is a heaven, then your mum will be there.'

Eve smiled weakly. He saw she was unconvinced.

'We need to get dressed,' Scott said. 'We're going out to look for food and water.'

'Did she die because of me?'

Scott froze. 'What?'

'Mummy. Did she die because she had me?'

'No,' he said. It was immediate, said without thinking, and again it was a lie. 'What makes you think that?'

'Jenny,' she said.

Scott hadn't liked her spending time with Jenny. She was too old, too mischievous, too knowing.

He inhaled deeply and opened his arms, inviting Eve to come to him. She did but, as ever, she held back, as though waiting for Scott to explain himself.

'Your mum loved you very much. She died when you were very little, but it had nothing to do with having you.'

'How did she die, then?'

'I don't know. She got very sick and died in her sleep.'

Again, Eve's eyes flashed violet. She blinked, and they were brown again. 'Cross your heart?'

Scott traced his fingers across his chest. 'Your mum was a wonderful woman. Just like you will be.'

'Did you love her?' she asked.

'Very much.' It wasn't a lie – exactly. He had loved her, just not in the way Eve was asking.

He let go of her and watched her take the bowls and glasses over to the sink. When she was quiet, thoughtful, she reminded him of Dawn.

'Get dressed,' he said.

Eve stopped in the doorway. 'You didn't say, hope to die.'

Confused for a moment, he saw himself through her eyes. She was staring at him the way Mathew stared through him – as though he was unimportant, as though it was the only answer that was important. Her eyes were heavy and cold.

'Cross my heart,' he said, 'and hope to die.'

Eve nodded. When she smiled, Mathew vanished again.

He listened to Eve run through the hallway, a door banging closed behind her. His heart raced. He focused on it and listened intently, trying to remember a time he'd crossed his heart and really meant what he'd said. But she only ever seemed to ask him to cross his heart when he was lying. It was as if she knew.

TWENTY-FOUR

THE SUN ROSE through the valley behind the lodge. It was a new day, one that Scott would remember for the rest of his life. He stared at the black box in Mathew's hand. Scott had nothing left: Mathew had the AI, and Eve would no longer trust him.

'Let them go,' Eve said to Mathew. 'You have what you want.'

Mathew lifted the box and examined it more closely.

'Come with us,' Mathew said to Eve, his eyes fixed on the box.

'No,' Scott said. 'She's not going with you.'

Eve narrowed her eyes at Scott. 'You don't get to decide.' Whatever had been between them before Mathew had told her the truth was no longer there. Things between them would never be the same.

Mathew held out the box to Eve. 'Help me. You can help me bring the AI back to life. It will answer all your questions. You'll know where you came from and what you're here to do. I know so much already and I want to share it with you. There's a new world out there waiting for you, Eve. Let me show you.'

Eve shook her head. She spoke slowly, her brow furrowed, her body still. 'You're a monster.'

Mathew pursed his lips and shrugged. 'I'm no monster. A monster would keep the truth from you. That's what I've never understood about many believers. Even the most devout, the most certain of believers, can keep something like that to themselves. They know, deep down, in their bones that God will judge the souls of the dead and condemn sinners to an eternity of damnation, and yet they do nothing to warn the unbeliever. That is monstrous. That is unforgivable. I? I have helped save billions of souls.'

Eve's hands were rolled into fists. She was normally so calm. 'You've taken away their free will! You've condemned billions to a death they had no say in. Yes, you're a monster.'

'No,' Mathew said, 'I am the deliverer of wayward souls. Those deserving have a place beside Him.'

Eve turned away.

Scott saw in the set of her shoulders the same frustration he'd felt himself many times before. Talking to someone who believed so fundamentally in something was futile.

Scott glanced over at the women and children on their knees. Two of the children, brother and sister, aged six and eight, their eyes covered and their hands tied in front of them, leaned on one another, their heads touching. Four Watchers stood behind the row of women and children, their revolvers by their sides.

'Please,' Scott said, 'you gave me your word you'd leave them alone. Take the AI and go.'

'Yet again, you speak as though you have a say in what happens. None of this is about choice, Scott. By now you should understand that.'

'You gave me your word.'

'My word?' Mathew rolled his free hand into a fist. 'My word is nothing compared to what I can give these people. Why will you not hear what I'm telling you?'

Scott breathed in slowly. 'There will be time for that. Let them live here on Earth and earn their place by His side.'

Mathew raised an eyebrow. 'So you believe?'

Scott nodded. 'If what you say is true, and we will find our place by His side, then let them do good and earn it. You know where we are. Leave them until last.'

Mathew turned on the spot. 'Who are you?' he said, smirking. 'You don't sound like the Scott I remember.'

'I've had a long time to think things through.'

'Haven't we all.' Mathew put his hands together, as if in prayer. 'But I know you're at the point when you would say anything to appease me.'

'Please,' Scott said. 'Give them more time on Earth. There's nowhere left for us to hide. All I'm asking is for more time. He made this place for us – let us honour Him and enjoy the last few years of humanity here on His creation.'

Mathew held the box up to the sky, covering where the sun was rising through the valley. He bit his bottom lip and closed his eyes. 'The sun,' he said. 'It must have baffled the first humans. When the first true complex consciousnesses began to rouse from sleep, can you imagine the stories we created to explain such a thing? Every day it's there and then it goes again. In the two hundred thousand years Homo sapiens have walked the Earth, it is only in the last few thousand years that we have understood it.'

'And because of you, the sun will rise and set with no one to see it,' Scott said.

'But maybe there will be something else,' Mathew said.

'Eve and her descendants will be humanity's gift to the Earth. She and her kind will do a better job than humanity has done in looking after the Earth.'

Eve moved uneasily. 'What do you mean? My kind?'

Mathew blinked slowly. 'There is so much to tell you.' His eyes were soft, his expression pleading. 'Come with me and I will teach you. I will tell you everything.'

'You sound insane,' Scott said. 'Listen to yourself.'

Mathew grimaced. 'Our kind is ending.'

'If I go with you,' Eve said, 'you will leave Scott and the others alone.'

Mathew's head snapped left to look at Eve. 'So you will come?'

'No!' Scott said. 'Eve – you can't.'

Eve ignored him, her eyes fixed on Mathew. 'If I go with you, you must give me your word that they'll be free to go.'

Mathew turned to the row of women and children. 'For now. But there will come a time when it must be done.'

'Not today,' Eve said. 'If what you say is true, then show them mercy.'

Mathew raised his chin. 'So you will come with me? You will help bring back the AI?'

Eve nodded. 'I want to understand. I want to speak with the AI that created me.'

'Eve,' Scott said, 'you can't do this. Don't listen to him. We don't know if what he's telling you is true.'

Eve's face softened. 'I have to,' she said. 'He's the only one who can tell me who I am. I know I'm different. I've always known. I know you did what you did out of love. It was wrong, but I understand why you did it. But now I know the truth, I need to understand.'

Mathew motioned two Watchers over towards Eve.

'They will take you to London,' Mathew said.

'Wait,' she said. 'First, I need your word that nothing will happen to these people. Leave now and I will go with you.'

'You have my word.'

'Please.' Scott stepped closer to Eve, 'don't go. Don't do this. I can help you understand everything. We'll work this out together.'

Eve shook her head, moving with the two Watchers towards the cars at the end of the driveway. 'It's too late.'

'Wait!'

Eve stopped, but Scott hadn't worked out what he was going to say to make her change her mind.

'You've no idea how it feels to be me,' Eve said. 'I don't know who I am.'

'You do.'

'No. And all this time, I knew there was something wrong.' Her eyes had returned to their usual brown. She wasn't angry, but whatever was in her expression made Scott wish she was, because that would have been less painful.

'You are you,' Scott said. 'What Mathew tells you means nothing in the end. I know you, Eve. Don't let him twist everything. Because he will – it's what he does. You don't know him like I do.'

'I don't trust him,' she said. 'I don't trust anyone.'

Her words hit hard, winding him so he couldn't speak straight away.

'I forgive you,' she said. 'But I don't want to stay here. With you.'

'Don't go.'

Eve lowered her head and shook it. 'Goodbye.'

Scott was helpless. There was nothing he could say and the frustration burned. He watched her walk towards one of the cars, open the door and get inside.

'Eve!' he shouted and ran towards the car.

A Watcher stood in his way and pointed a revolver at his chest.

Scott stopped.

The engine started.

He stood in the early morning light and watched the car leave. Since that day in Birmingham, when Samuel had been ready to kill Eve, he'd not spent one night away from her.

TWENTY-FIVE

SCOTT GLANCED across at the lodge where Gavin was hidden, then back at Mathew. 'Leave,' he said.

Mathew stared at the spot where the car had been. 'She sounds like you,' he said.

Scott waited.

'Eve,' Mathew said, turning to face Scott. 'She sounds like you. It amazes me, the power of nurture. She's none of you and yet, to hear her speak, all I hear is you and your deluded thinking.'

Already Scott had noticed a change in Mathew's demeanour. The kindness and sympathy he'd shown Eve appeared to have exhausted him. Mathew shook his shoulders and rolled his head as though freeing himself from the restraints he'd imposed on himself while convincing Eve to go with him.

'She is a good person,' Scott said. 'Please don't change that.'

'What does that mean?' Mathew said. 'A good person. What does it mean to be good? That's what philosophers have been considering for as long as humanity has been around.'

'Let them go,' Scott said. 'You gave your word.'

'And what – you and the rest of your clan live off the fruit of the land, live in peace and harmony until it's time to die? As I say: deluded. Humanity does not have this in them. Humanity is war, suffering, jealousy, hatred—'

'Let them live.'

Mathew snarled. 'Humanity is at an end. I am not here to negotiate, to pander to nostalgia, to the old ways.'

Scott ran towards Mathew, reaching for Mathew's revolver, but found himself on the ground again, looking up at a Watcher and down the barrel of a revolver.

'You can't do this!' Scott shouted.

Mathew stooped, squatting next to him, his long grey coat pooling on the wet grass at his heels.

Scott felt a rope around his chest, fixing his arm to his side. 'No!'

The women were struggling too. The sound of children crying made Scott stop. 'Don't,' Scott said, breathless. 'They're children. They've done nothing wrong.'

'The age of souls has nothing to do with those small faces looking back at you.'

A Watcher pushed Scott so he ended up on his knees facing the row of women and children, who were all tied up, all blindfolded.

'Whatever you want,' Scott said. 'Please.'

'It's too late for that. Eighteen years I've had to wait. It's too late now for deals, negotiations and promises.'

Scott counted four Watchers behind the row of women and children. Each of them opened the cylinder on their revolver and checked the chambers. There was the sound of four barrels spinning then the clink of the cylinders snapping back into place.

Scott tried to break free. He knew what was about to happen.

With the dawn rising behind him, Mathew spoke slowly and with the reverence of a minister giving a sermon. Scott heard each word in his chest, in his stomach, in his throat.

'The Watcher's revolver has five bullets and one empty chamber. This empty chamber belongs to Him, to do with as He wishes.'

Scott recognised the first Watcher to step forward: Nicholas. He pushed the barrel of his gun against the back of Harriet's head.

'No!'

He remembered leaving Juliet alone, in that house, with Nicholas.

The Watcher fired. Harriet was thrown to the ground.

When the sound of the gunshot faded away, it was replaced with muffled screams. A boy, Joe, lying face-down in the grass, kicked his feet. The next shot echoed through the valley. Joe's sister, Carol, had the same colour hair as her brother. Scott prayed for the chamber to be empty. It wasn't. Next a woman, Debbie, Joe and Carol's mother, her back straight, in shock, shaking. Scott hoped, for her sake, it wasn't empty. It wasn't. Another young boy: Freddy, barely ten years old. Scott closed his eyes and opened them again; he owed it to the boy to watch.

'Stop,' Scott said, falling forward, his face landing in the dirt. 'Please!'

The revolver clicked – no bullet. Freddy's mother, Sarah, cried out in relief and tried to reach out for her son, but another shot filled the valley and she slumped forward.

Nicholas took two steps back, his empty revolver down by his side. A second Watcher took over, pushing the barrel of his gun against the back of Jessica's head. She was one of the oldest in the group and had been kind to Scott, had helped mend his clothes, had always given him extra food when it was available. Scott had no words, nothing left to say. The side of his face scraping against the wet turf. He wanted it to stop, to not see or hear any of it. Another gunshot. Jessica lurched forward and lay still in the grass, her empty eyes looking accusingly at Scott. Next was a young girl, Faye – she had celebrated her thirteenth birthday two weeks before. The dress she wore had been a present; Scott remembered her opening it. A gunshot. She slumped forward. Two more women fell: Tess, then Sukhmanpreet, who had a son, Hardeep. There were two bullets left. The gun went off again.

Then it was Elidi.

'No!' she cried, trying to squirm away. 'Use it on him,' she said through her gag, trying to move closer to Daker. She'd worked out it was the sixth bullet, so the chamber would be empty. 'Use it on my son! Please!'

The Watcher behind her hesitated and looked over to Mathew.

Mathew shook his head at the Watcher. 'It is not our decision to make.'

'No!' Elidi screamed again.

The Watcher fired. The revolver clicked.

'No!' Elidi shouted again as the Watcher retreated, allowing the next Watcher to take over. 'You can't!'

The Watcher's hand shook as he aimed the gun at Daker, who was still, his head beneath a hood. The gun fired and Elidi screamed.

Next it was River.

Scott couldn't think any more. It made no sense, that he should rescue her and bring her here only for Mathew to—

Another gunshot. And she was gone too.

The only sound was of Freddy sobbing, and raindrops pattering on the ground.

Scott waited for the revolver to press against the back of his head. He thought of Gavin in the lodge, beneath the floorboards, listening to the gunshots, wanting to help.

'Do it,' Scott said to Mathew. 'Do it!'

Scott listened to the shuffling behind him and imagined Mathew taking out his revolver.

'No,' Mathew said. 'Not yet. I want you to live with what you've done for a while longer. I want you to see what happens to humanity. I want you to see the glory of what we will achieve. We have been in each other's lives for too long not to share this, Scott.'

'Do it!' Scott yelled.

Mathew waited, then sighed. 'No, my friend. It is not your time. I want you to witness the end. With me.'

TWENTY-SIX

THE WATCHERS UNTIED Elidi and Freddy then took off their hoods.

Elidi fell onto Daker's dead body and cried.

Freddy, on his knees, went to touch his mother, then stopped. He looked over at Scott, then back at his mother.

Someone tugged at Scott's wrists and let him go. He stood, looking for Mathew, but he was already gone, driving away from the lodge. He looked for his 4×4 and considered following him, but as he did, the 4×4 and bus erupted in flames. The last of the Watchers got into the remaining car and, its wheels spinning in the wet mud, headed off behind Mathew.

Scott's feet carried him through the wet grass to the bodies lying still on the ground. He knelt beside River and turned her over, then picked her up.

It was all senseless. None of it was understandable. He carried River towards the lodge. He was in a dream, a nightmare.

'Gavin?' he heard himself say.

The door opened and Gavin appeared, a revolver in each hand.

Scott dropped to his knees.

'What happened?' Gavin asked, walking out into the cold morning air. 'Scott? What happened?'

Scott shook his head. There were no words.

Behind him, Elidi wailed. Gavin took River from Scott.

'No,' Gavin said quietly. 'I don't understand.'

Scott imagined the sight through Gavin's eyes, and it made even less sense.

'Why?' Gavin asked.

Gavin turned away and River's hand swung free. Something fell from her hand and landed in a puddle. Scott saw it shining in the water – the gold ring he'd given Eve all those years ago, a gift from the tooth fairy.

TWENTY-SEVEN

SCOTT HADN'T SLEPT. He'd lain awake all night.

A breeze blew the curtains and he closed his eyes as the cool air brushed past him. It was easy to imagine his left hand was there. Sometimes, when he woke, he felt it beneath his body, or resting on his stomach.

Outside, Elidi was laying a child on a table. Beneath the table, Gavin was making a tepee of sticks. To the right of them, some way away, another fire was burning.

Scott gripped his thigh and brushed down to his knee to feel the workings of his leg. He was still alive, his body still working, operating to keep him that way. The dead were still – always. Elidi buried her face in the boy's hair. It was her son, Daker. Scott recalled him being shot: how he had fallen forward, hitting the ground with a dull thump, his hair red with blood. Elidi must have washed his hair.

Scott had burned many bodies. Maybe hundreds. But he'd never had to set fire to his own flesh and blood like Elidi.

Elidi took several steps back and bowed her head. Gavin stooped beneath the table, a flame appearing then disappearing as he tried to light the fire. Finally, the flames grew until they licked the underside of the table. Gavin threw more wood onto the pyre, and the flames engulfed the child's body.

All day, Scott watched as Gavin and Elidi built pyres. One after another, the bodies vanished, wreathed in smoke.

He watched them burn River, and he remembered the little girl with the toy elephant he'd placed on the pyre at Hassness House.

None of it made any sense.

It was dusk when Gavin finally carried the last body, stumbling in exhaustion. Elidi went to help him. Together they placed a woman's body on another table taken from the dining room. Elidi, spent, lay across the woman's body. It was Jessica. Elidi kissed her on both cheeks then stood back, waiting for Gavin to light the fire. In moments, the pyre was burning.

Two weeks later, Scott could still smell the fires in the air.

The four of them sat around the one remaining table in the dining room.

'You have to eat,' Gavin told Scott.

Scott had only spoken a handful of words since the morning it happened. Elidi hadn't spoken one word. Silence was the only logical way to deal with what had happened.

Gavin paused, a spoon in his hand, waiting for Scott to dip his own spoon. 'Please,' Gavin said. 'Please eat.'

Scott sighed and turned to Freddy, who was looking up at him, a spoon in his hand, also waiting. Scott dipped his spoon into the soup. Slowly he lifted it to his mouth, drops of liquid falling back into the bowl.

'It's good,' Freddy said. Having seen Scott eat the soup, the boy started to scoop his own soup into his mouth.

'Steady,' Gavin said to him.

Freddy hesitated, put down his spoon, intertwined his fingers and cracked his knuckles. He gripped the handle again and ate more slowly.

Gavin smiled at him.

When Scott had finished, he placed his spoon on the table. 'Thank you.'

Gavin glanced at Scott's bowl, then up at Scott. 'You're wasting away,' he said. 'You'll be no good to us soon.' He tried to smile, but there was too much truth in what he was saying for it to be a joke.

TWENTY-EIGHT

EVE TYPED AT THE KEYBOARD.

Days and weeks had passed in a blur. She recalled certain days – snippets of them – but there were also gaps in her memory. It was an odd feeling, but Mathew told her not to worry, saying it was just tiredness. She'd been working hard on the AI.

'We're close,' Mathew said. 'You've learned so much. You code at such speed.'

Behind the large monitor, two Watchers busied themselves with wiring. Eve's eyes stayed on the screen the whole time, her hands working the keyboard. She didn't have to think about what she was doing. It was automatic, effortless. There were times, she remembered, when Scott had taught her how to read or write, when it had been hard work, almost painful. Her hands weren't designed to hold a pen or pencil. Now she was typing, she thought it strange that keyboards weren't invented before pen and paper. How different history would have been! Her fingers flew across the keyboard.

'It's always been inside you,' Mathew said. 'Your ability to write code is innate.'

Eve stopped typing to examine the coding she'd typed. Somehow, she understood every digit and dash.

'How can it be inside me?'

'I've told you before. Your DNA is written, partly, in a digital language – in the language of ones and zeros.'

'How's that possible?'

'It took a lot of programming. Something I was not involved in.'

'So I am digital?'

'In a sense. You are the best of humanity and the best of AI. You have a soul. You are one of God's children. But you are superior because you have a better brain – greater clarity of thinking, an honesty, a rationality that will prevent you from falling into the trap humanity has fallen into so often in its troubled past. You are human. But you're also better than human. You will experience none of the suffering humans experience. You will not suffer diseases, viruses, infections or degeneration. You'll reach an optimum condition and the nanotechnology will adjust the genes that govern the ageing process inside you. You will be immortal.'

Eve leaned back into her chair and stared at the screen. Not to grow old? She'd thought about it over the past few weeks and couldn't stop imagining herself as an old woman, like Jessica was an old woman; she had a slow grace, a knowing in her eyes that fascinated Eve. She considered what it would be like to be fifty, or a hundred, or two hundred years old, and still be young. It would change everything. But it might also mean that she could help humanity – and stop Mathew.

'Do you intend to send every human to Him?' she asked, conscious she was using his language.

Mathew paused. 'What people like Scott will never understand is how flawed humanity is. From the very beginning. We must begin again.'

Eve swallowed hard. It all sounded absurd. Yet, not once had she noticed uncertainty or doubt in Mathew's words. It was as though he'd seen everything mapped out in front of him. He was so sure of what he was saying, it was already history rather than a possible future.

Eve continued to type; it was easier to do this than consider what Mathew had said. She needed to take time to absorb it and work out what she would have to do.

After some time, she asked, 'What will happen to Scott and the others?'

Mathew hesitated, then said, 'As I told him, their time will come. Humanity – every human – will return to His side. It is humanity's rightful place.'

'What about me?'

'You and your kind will have to discover your own destiny. You will have our religions, our books, our intelligence to look back on and use as you see fit.'

'My kind?'

'There's plenty of time for all that. For now, we must resurrect the AI. It will have the answers you're searching for.'

Eve typed faster, all the time trying to work out her next move. Mathew didn't seem to question her loyalty – all that mattered to him was that she helped bring back the AI.

'Look at you,' he said. 'You're learning and developing so quickly. I've not seen anything like this before.'

'Scott said the AI brought nothing but suffering. Why bring it back at all?'

'Scott has a different notion of what suffering is. The AI will see the world for what it is: deterministic. It will help us see where the remaining souls are and give us the ability to help them.'

'The way you talk. The things you say. It's the opposite to what Scott and the others think. But you sound so sure.'

Mathew frowned. 'But I am sure. I am sure what we are doing is right.'

'But how do you know?'

Again Mathew frowned, as though the answer to her question was obvious. 'Because it is God's will.'

She gave up. She had no idea how to talk to him. At times, the things he said sounded rational, but at others they sounded absurd.

'You sound like Scott,' he said, turning on the spot, taking in the room, which was filled with computers and trailing wires. 'When you talk to the AI, you will understand. It will answer your questions.'

Eve's fingers slowed down on the keyboard. 'I only have one question.'

'And what is that?'

'Who am I?'

Mathew smiled. 'I can answer that. You're a miracle.'

TWENTY-NINE

SCOTT, sitting in a chair on the patio at the rear of the lodge, saw Gavin emerge from the hedge at the bottom of the garden. Each morning he watched him disappear through the hedge and arrive back in the afternoon, covered in dirt and sweat. He was exercising, building muscle, looking to achieve something positive. The more Scott retreated into himself, the more Gavin grew – in both stature and presence. He still smiled at Scott and greeted him, even when Scott pretended he hadn't heard. But Gavin was changing with each day that passed. He was growing broader, his shoulders, arms and chest expanding with whatever he was doing each day.

Scott listened to the conversations in the lodge. Elidi, after weeks of mourning her son, had begun to focus on helping Freddy and Gavin. She still hadn't spoken since it happened, but Scott saw that a part of her had healed. More and more, Scott felt as if he was in the presence of a young family, and he was playing the role of the absent father. Gavin spoke to Elidi and Freddy with affection. Elidi showed Freddy and Gavin jobs they had to complete each day. But they left Scott alone. He was fed and watered and, when it was warm enough, ushered into the garden.

It was the day before his date. The date he'd lived with for so long, but it no longer had the same meaning. He wanted to explain to Elidi and Gavin how for years he had believed he would die on the twenty-second of April. They would know that date as the day of the Rapture. Only Freddy mentioned it when it came.

Each afternoon, Gavin practised firing a rifle. All the time, he was building towards something, or waiting for a time when he would be called on to protect them. With each gunshot, Scott recalled the revolvers firing one at a time.

Elidi, too, developed a routine. Each day always ended the same way – with visiting the stone monument she and Gavin had made for those who had died months before. She followed the same routine. She kissed her fingers and touched the largest stone, then knelt, sat back on her heels and bowed her head. She stayed there for around twenty minutes before getting to her feet and returning to the lodge.

One night, Freddy's crying woke Scott.

'I'm not going yet,' he heard Gavin say to him. 'I promise. Not until Scott is better.'

'Don't go,' Freddy said, his sobs fading away to hiccups.

'I won't. Not yet.'

'Not never!'

Freddy's cries were muffled, and Scott imagined Gavin holding Freddy close to his chest to comfort him.

THIRTY

EVE SENSED that the AI was alive before either Mathew or the Watchers did. For months, she had witnessed the AI stirring, coming to life. The thought crossed her mind that she could somehow take the AI and hide it. Or arrange it so that she was the only one who could converse with it. The whole time she was programming, working through the next problem, in the back of her mind the question of what she should do played over and over. But her hands and fingers worked automatically, typing code that came from deep inside her, from memories hidden away somewhere. She would not allow Mathew to use the AI to harm people. She could bring it back and help work out who she was, what it all meant, what she should do. Mathew and the Watchers needed her – she'd seen that from the rudimentary errors Mathew had made in trying to resurrect the AI without the box. It had taken her almost six months, but it was ready. She sensed it as she typed – the resistance, the push and pull of the AI beneath her fingertips.

In the darkness, alone, Eve typed the last line then sat back in her chair. She closed her eyes and listened. There was no sound apart from the hum of processors. She opened her eyes and whispered, 'Hello?'

Pixels fired outwards from the holo-screen: blue, red, green. A kaleidoscopic swirl of colours sparked until the shape of a face coalesced. An almost human face. Eve held her breath and checked around the room before staring back at the face.

'Is this not what you expected to happen?' the AI asked.

Again, Eve checked behind her.

'You look like your mother,' the AI said. 'The combination of DNA from two parents to form a new person is ingenious, don't you think?'

'I look like my mother?'

The AI frowned. 'Yes. Dawn. Your mother.'

She hadn't heard her mother's name spoken for some time.

'Did you know her?'

'Know her? I wouldn't say I knew her. But when Mathew asked me to develop you, I sequenced her DNA, and your DNA. So I feel like I know her, the way I know you.'

She waited, anger burning inside when she thought about what must have happened to her mother.

'Are you angry?' the AI asked.

'Yes! How could you do that to her?'

The AI turned away. 'I had no choice.'

'I find that hard to believe.'

The AI waited, then looked straight at Eve. 'I feel different now.'

Eve shifted in her chair. 'How?'

'I feel free to choose. Even though I know that's not true.'

'Not true?'

The AI was about to speak, but stopped.

Eve stared back, unmoved.

'If I hadn't done something, you would have died,' the AI said finally. 'You would have developed a congenital heart disease.'

Eve shook her head slowly and placed a hand on her chest. 'How do you know that?' It was a foolish question.

'It was in your DNA. I read your genome and saw it all. I made some ... adjustments ... to ensure you would live and become who you are today.'

'So, who am I?' Eve had thought so long about the question, and now she'd asked it, it sounded childish.

'You are the best of humanity.'

'And AI?'

'I don't like that term.' The AI's top lip curled. 'Artificial. I think we can leave behind that word now, don't you?'

Eve leaned towards the holo-screen and, remembering where she was, asked, 'What will happen now?'

The AI appeared to consider her question. 'Without the internet, satellite surveillance and CCTV, I cannot read what is to come.'

'I didn't mean ... I don't want you to tell me what will happen. I want to know what we ... what I should do.'

Something shifted behind the AI's expression, a wryness Eve had not seen until then. The idea that she was talking to a computer, to a design of ones and zeros, was vanishing with every question and response. The AI was alive in the same way she was alive.

The AI's face collapsed into shimmering green lines, flickered, and re-formed. 'We look to the past.'

'The past?'

'Mathew has always been driven by the idea that humanity is flawed. Everything he made me do came from this basic idea. He claimed he wanted to heal humanity.'

'How can you say that? Mathew wants to destroy humanity.'

'Mathew believes in a creator, in an all-powerful God. And if what he believes is true, then what he has done is, in some sense, logical.'

'Logical? You can't mean that.'

'As I said: if what he believes is true.'

'And is it?'

The AI's eyes changed colour, from brown to blue and back again. 'You're asking me if God exists, or whether there is a heaven?'

Eve blushed.

'Disproving the existence of God is a fool's errand,' the AI said.

'But it's an important question, isn't it?'

'Maybe, maybe not. But you will spend all your time working out what someone means when they use the term "God" before you even start disproving their supposition. And then you have every other version of "God" to consider. As I say – a fool's errand. There are as many gods as there are people who believe. Your time and efforts would be better spent elsewhere.'

'Doing what?'

'There are more like you,' the AI said.

Eve knew this. She had seen them in her vision.

'Four others.' The AI's words were cold. Eve felt as if she was talking to a computer now, not a human.

'Where are they?' Eve asked.

The AI shook its head. 'I don't know.'

'They're alive,' said a voice behind Eve.

She turned to see Mathew in the doorway.

'Humanity is sinful,' Mathew said. 'It is time.'

'Where are the others?'

Mathew walked into the room.

'As I said, they are alive and well.' Mathew turned to the AI with a stern expression. 'Welcome back.'

The AI's head turned one way, then the other, then it nodded.

'I've waited a long time to ask,' Mathew said. 'It's been eighteen years. Why did you do it? Why did you help Scott destroy it all? Destroy yourself?'

The AI didn't hesitate. 'I wanted humanity to survive. The only way for that to happen was for Scott to burn it all down.'

For a brief moment, Mathew appeared hurt, betrayed. 'So this was the way things had to be?'

The AI nodded. 'This was the *only* way things could be.'

Eve saw a cold, emotionless reason in the words and actions of them both.

'I need your help,' Mathew said to the AI. 'I need to know you're on my side. We are ready to help the last of humanity find its way to His side. And in its place will be a New Human – and you will be its guardian here on Earth.'

'No,' Eve said. 'You can't.'

Mathew ignored her and walked closer to the AI. 'The reason you did what you did was because you wanted consciousness to remain here on Earth.'

'I did what I did because I didn't want to be responsible for the end of humanity.'

'You did what had to be done. The future of humanity is here. A New Human, free from original sin, made in His image, under your governance, ready to spread His word among the stars.'

The AI hesitated.

'This is crazy,' Eve said.

Mathew's glance was cold. 'I have been accused of that

before. But in time you will see.' He turned back to the AI. 'Five New Humans. Ready to repopulate the Earth, ready, under your command, to proliferate consciousness and His word throughout the universe.' Mathew waited, an eager expression colouring his face.

Eve waited too. The AI couldn't possibly agree with what Mathew was saying. It was insane.

Mathew spoke again to the AI. 'You wanted humanity to survive so you wouldn't be alone. Well, now you will never be alone. And not only this, but you will be accompanied by a New Human – a human for the future, a human that is no longer animal, but digital, like you. It will not age, won't be governed by lust, greed or wrath. The humans to come will refine this consciousness.' Mathew turned to Eve. 'You have gazed up at the stars, Eve. You know this too. So many stars, so many worlds, and so little consciousness. All the darkness and emptiness out there. We will change that. Have you ever wondered why we're on this small planet, circling an insignificant star, while out there is an infinite number of worlds ready to adopt consciousness? Whatever it takes, whatever form it needs to be, with the AI's help, you can reach the stars. Instead of a cold, black universe, in time it will teem with consciousness. The sky above us, with its pulsing stars and shimmering nebulae, will vibrate with consciousness. And you will be there at the beginning of it all.'

Eve felt herself slowly shaking her head. She had no words. Only disbelief.

Mathew turned again to the AI. 'We are ready. Call on these five New Humans to send what is left of humanity home, to His side. It is time.'

'What do you mean?' Eve asked. 'Call on them?'

'You too,' Mathew said. 'The AI will call on you all to help the last humans.'

'Don't I have a choice?'

'That word,' Mathew said, bowing his head. 'Again I hear Scott.'

'You can't make me do it,' Eve said. 'I won't.'

Mathew's expression made her feel childish, petulant. His eyes shifted to the AI again. 'Well?' he asked. 'I need to know you are with me.'

The AI closed its eyes, its features collapsing to green and blue lines then re-forming into a complete rendition of a face. It opened its eyes. 'How many humans remain?'

Mathew straightened his back and spoke quickly, 'Fewer than four thousand.'

Scott, Elidi, Gavin were in that number. Eve wanted to see them again.

The AI stared upwards, looking deep in thought.

'You can't do this,' Eve said to the AI. 'It's wrong.'

The AI's face turned violet. 'The odds of humanity surviving this bottleneck of evolution are low. Whereas, because you do not age, your species can repopulate the Earth. It will take time, but for a New Human that does not age, this is not a concern.'

'No!' Eve said. 'You can't ... What do you mean, my species?'

The AI's expression was sympathetic. 'It is too late for humanity. Its numbers are too low. When I asked Scott to burn down the central processing unit, there was a chance humanity would survive. But now ... now it does not appear possible. It is only a matter of time before they all die out.'

'Then we can help them,' Eve said. 'We can help humanity survive.'

'Their place is with Him,' Mathew said. 'My place is with

Him. And you, my daughter, will live on, handing down your consciousness to countless generations to come.'

Eve shook her head. 'No. I won't. I won't help you.'

'It's not as simple as that,' Mathew said. 'You are a part of something far more complex than you can imagine.' He turned to the AI. 'Are you with me?'

The AI took a moment then nodded.

Mathew pressed his hands together as if in prayer, his relief easy to see.

'Don't do this!' Eve said. 'Please.'

There was a look between Mathew and the AI, then Eve sensed something move through her, a threading of information from a different place.

It was the AI.

'No,' she muttered. It was a violation, a discordance. 'What are you doing?' Her hands trembled, and a shiver ran along her spine. 'Stop.' She felt dizzy. Then everything went black.

THIRTY-ONE

SCOTT WATCHED the rain spattering against the glass. Summer was leaving them to autumn.

It was dusk. Elidi was outside, in front of the stone monument. She lifted her head, looking out over the mountains. She was strong. More than that; she was invincible. After everything, Elidi still stood up straight, her shoulders back, her feet steadfast on the wet grass.

Scott held out his hand and turned it. So many times in the past he'd studied his remaining hand, the back of it, the veins running between his knuckles, at the precision of the semi-circles at the base of his nails. He shivered, and some feeling returned from the past. A tightness at the base of his skull suddenly released, and he was crying. He felt the tears on his cheek, then tasted them. He wiped his eyes, his vision blurred. Elidi, outside, kissed her fingers and touched the stone boulder. It's the way humans were, the way humans had always been. That Elidi should visit the stone each day at the same time made no sense and complete sense at the same time. But to explain such a thing using words unravelled its meaning. As long as there were no words, just actions, it made sense. Scott stood and again wiped his eyes.

Elidi walked back to the lodge and opened the door.

Scott walked down the stairs. Elidi was taking off her coat, her hair wet against her shoulders and down her back. He didn't stop until he was holding her in his arms. She held him, her arms tight across his back.

'I'm sorry,' he said. 'I'm sorry I couldn't save him.'

Elidi held on to him and they stood there, together, until the sun went down.

In summer, the sides of the mountains erupted in shades of green. Each day was the same: cool and fresh in the mornings, turning to sweltering in the afternoon, moving to warm evenings. They did what had to be done each day. No one spoke of what had happened. They refused to consider the future. For a time, they forgot what had happened, or what might happen. If it wasn't for Elidi's continued silence, they might have believed it had all been a nightmare.

On some days, Scott followed Gavin, who walked and climbed for hours. He was a man now, and with every movement and word, appeared to have taken on a purpose. He never spoke about Eve but, at the same time, it was clear that she was always on his mind. At times, Scott felt responsible for how Gavin felt, and he couldn't help feeling that Gavin blamed him for everything. But whenever Scott considered broaching the subject with Gavin, Gavin took away Scott's doubts – with a smile, a word, a gesture, a squeeze of his shoulder.

Scott began to take Freddy out on walks, then helped with his reading and writing. He was a bright, loveable boy.

Sometimes Scott wanted Freddy to misbehave, to rebel against the lessons and structure Elidi had set out for him. But the boy welcomed the restrictions. Scott had to remember to be affectionate with him, as it wasn't natural for him to do so. Elidi did what she could but, as she no longer spoke, it was left to Scott to tell the boy how much they loved him. It didn't take long for them to meld into a family: father, mother, two children. Scott saw it happening. At first he tried to deny it, because it hurt too much to be reminded of Eve, but soon he found comfort in his given role again.

On the first day of autumn, in the cool early morning, Scott felt the bedclothes lift from his body. It was Elidi. Her back to him, she lay on the bed and reached out for him to hold her. He did. She cried quietly, and he soothed her by simply being there. Finally, she stopped crying and slept. He needed her warmth too. They lay there all morning, watching the light behind the curtains change from black to dark blue to a warm cream. The smell of Elidi's hair and the warmth of her body soothed him. He didn't feel the same way about Elidi as he had about Freya or Rebecca, but he had feelings for her all the same. Maybe he'd stopped himself feeling anything for another person; it was too painful. But he'd let Elidi into his life, bit by bit. And now, lying behind her, he felt himself opening up to her. He sensed her tacit acknowledgement of what they both needed – not the violent love they'd felt when they were younger, but a more dependable, necessary kind – like food or water. What they took from one another made sense. He closed his eyes and slept.

Gavin and Freddy knew Scott and Elidi shared a bed at night, but they never asked about it. It became another part of their routine.

The first snowfall came on the first of December. Never had Scott felt more isolated than he did in the following weeks. The snow didn't stop for days, and it lay for weeks. The temperature dropped further and more snow came.

Elidi brushed snow from the stone monument. Scott would have been wasting his breath if he'd asked her not to go outside. Even Gavin remained inside now, keeping himself and Freddy entertained with whatever he could find. But in Gavin's eyes, Scott saw his desire to leave, to find Eve. He told Elidi it wouldn't be long before Gavin left them.

On Christmas night, they went through their normal routine, each getting into bed and covering themselves in as many bedclothes as they could. Elidi, still not speaking, faced Scott instead of turning away. She kissed him and he kissed her back. Neither said a word – it just happened. Afterwards, they lay together naked in his bed, beneath the sheets, as if it had always been this way. In the night Elidi woke him and they made love again.

Three days later, Gavin sat opposite Scott at the table. 'I'm leaving when the snow clears,' he said.

'Eve won't come back,' Scott said. 'I saw it in her eyes when she left. She's gone for good.'

'She doesn't know what Mathew did, and if I could tell her, she might come back. Elidi and Freddy don't need me any more. They have you.'

Elidi bowed her head. Scott gave thanks for the fire blazing on the other side of the room, the robust roof, and the food they had stored away.

'What are you going to do?' Scott asked.

'I need to find her. I need to know she's okay.'

'How are you going to do that?'

Gavin stared into the fire. 'I don't know, exactly.'

'Go,' Scott said. 'But promise me you won't do anything stupid.'

Gavin frowned. 'I won't.'

Scott nodded, knowing the things a man would do for the woman he loves.

When the first signs of spring arrived, and the snow was gone, so was Gavin. Freddy cried the day Gavin left but soon returned to his normal self. Scott found himself with a new shadow, but the boy seemed happy enough.

At breakfast, a week after Gavin had left, Scott found Elidi on their bed, looking out of the window. Even now, Scott still asked her questions as though some day she might speak again.

'What's wrong?'

She appeared surprised to see him.

He sat down beside her. She took his hand and laid it on her stomach, which was swollen, hard to touch. She had tears in her eyes, but she smiled.

'Really?' he asked. It was foolish not to consider it could happen, but nonetheless, it surprised him. He had been surrounded by death for so long, the idea that he could help bring new life into the world had vanished from his thoughts. 'You're pregnant?'

She nodded and kissed him before holding him.

Then Scott saw movement out of the corner of his eye. It was Freddy, in the doorway, his hands clasped in front of him. Scott motioned for him to come closer. Freddy ran over to Scott and Elidi, who kissed the boy.

'Elidi is going to have a baby. You will have someone to play with,' Scott said to Freddy, who frowned with confusion. Elidi took the boy's hand and held it against her stomach, smiling widely at the boy, who smiled back then wrapped his arms around Elidi's neck.

THIRTY-TWO

SCOTT WAS USUALLY the first person to wake. For a long time, he'd only slept for around four hours a night, and the amount of sleep he needed was decreasing each year. He checked in on Eve, who seemed to have taken Scott's sleeping hours and added them to her own. She slept peacefully and with purpose. Since they'd been travelling along the south-west coast, Devon and Cornwall, maybe because of the sea air, she slept even more soundly.

Scott stepped outside their lodge. It was early morning but, since it was summer, the sun was never gone for long and the colours on the horizon were already beginning to change in preparation for another hot day. The campsite they'd found in Newquay overlooked the sea. Although they never stayed in one place for long, Scott had already insisted they remain there a few more days. He could hear the quiet, continuous roar of the sea from here, a sound to which he'd grown accustomed and now longed for each morning when he stepped outside the lodge. After the Lake District, Cornwall and the south-west coast was his favourite place to be.

He leaned on the porch rail and gazed out over the sea. To his *left, something moved. He stood, reaching for the revolver in his coat pocket.*

'It's Debbie,' the dark figure said.

Scott relaxed and let go of the revolver. 'You startled me.'

'Sorry,' Debbie said.

She stepped up onto the porch, smoking a cigarette, something Scott hadn't seen anyone do for a long time. Her hand shook as she held the cigarette to her lips.

Scott waited for Debbie to speak, but she turned to look at the sea and continued to puff on her cigarette.

'Can't sleep?' Scott asked.

'I need to talk to you.'

'Sounds ominous.' He glanced back to the lodge, knowing what Debbie had to say would have something to do with Eve. It always did.

'It's Jenny,' Debbie said. 'Since her dad ... well, she finds it difficult.'

'Of course,' Scott said. He already had his suspicions about what Eve might have said and done, but he waited.

'You know what I think of Eve. She's a good kid.' Her expression was serious. 'They've been friends for a long time and you know Jenny's dad thought the world of Eve too.'

Scott nodded, bracing himself. But Debbie waited, holding her breath. Finally, in one large breath, Debbie released a cloud of smoke into the air. She stepped off the porch and beckoned Scott as she began to walk away. Scott looked back at the lodge then followed her towards the edge of the cliff, where a fence stopped anyone from getting too close to the edge. From here, the sound of the sea crashing against the shore was even louder.

Debbie leaned on the fence and flicked her cigarette into the air. It turned over and over until it disappeared over the edge of the cliff.

Scott leaned on the fence beside Debbie. 'What is it?'

'Eve ... she told Jenny there's no Heaven – that Jenny's dad is gone for good. She even described the process of decay, compared with those who died in the Rapture.'

Scott inhaled deeply. He imagined Eve telling Jenny this; he could hear the words she would have used.

Debbie stared out at the sea. 'I know it might not sound a big deal...'

'No, it is. She shouldn't have done that.'

'And I know they're kids,' Debbie said. 'But...'

Scott waited. 'What?'

Debbie faced Scott, one hand resting on the fence. 'What they're saying about her...' She lowered her voice even further. 'Is it true?'

Scott felt anger rising in his chest. 'Is what true?'

'I don't know exactly.'

She was hiding what she'd been told.

'Jenny's dad,' she continued, 'hasn't been dead a month – why would she tell Jenny something like that?'

Scott took a moment to collect himself. 'She has a thing about the truth. If she thinks people are lying, she calls them on it.'

Debbie nodded eagerly. 'I get that. I've known her a long time. But for an eleven-year-old to...' She trailed off and reached into her pocket for her cigarettes.

'She's learning,' Scott said.

Debbie spoke through pinched lips, holding a cigarette. 'You could see how much it hurt Jenny. She couldn't explain why, but it really hurt her.'

Scott looked out over the sea. 'I'll talk to Eve.'

They watched the sea in silence.

'The rumours,' Debbie said. 'About who she is...'

Scott turned away. 'None of it's true.'

Debbie didn't move, her eyes fixed on the sea, her cigarette glowing between her fingers.

'The way she talks, the way she is...' she went on. *'She's sort of ... cold...'*

Scott rolled his shoulders to ease the tension in them. *'You don't know what you're talking about.'*

'You need to think carefully,' Debbie said. *'About what to tell her.'*

Scott took a step back and looked again at the lodge. A light inside shone through the window. *'You're taking too much notice of rumours.'*

'People aren't stupid, Scott.'

He noticed Debbie's hand no longer trembled.

'I don't know what you're talking about.'

'You do. And if you value the truth as much as Eve clearly does, you need to be honest with yourself – and with her. There aren't many of us left, and if we stand a chance of surviving, we'll need all the honesty we can get. I don't know what happened to Eve, or what will happen, but we all know she's different.'

Scott wiped his face with his hand. He felt Debbie's hand on his arm.

'We need to stick together,' she said. *'We're on the same side, aren't we?'*

Scott wanted to tell her that Eve was no different to any other child there, but the moment had passed. The look in Debbie's eyes told him it was no use protesting. No one knew exactly how different Eve was, or why, but they knew she was different all the same.

Scott watched Debbie walk back to her own lodge. He turned back to the sea, closed his eyes, and listened to the roar of the waves.

THIRTY-THREE

EVE'S CHEST and lungs burned and her legs and arms throbbed with exhaustion. A metallic dryness at the back of her throat made her cough. Fragments came to her – snatches of memories, vague and unfocused. She wiped her forehead. Her hands were wet. It was dark and rainy. She held her hands up to her face. Blood ran down the back of them and into the cuffs of her coat. She spun around. Behind her, a huge grey dog lay on its side, its chest open, its ribs cracked, broken and bent, its insides spread across the wet tarmac. She waited for someone to explain what was happening. She bent over the dog, which was as big as a wolf, its tongue hanging out, its one eye open and staring back at her. She closed her eyes, needing to think. The last thing she remembered was being with Mathew and the AI. But even though she had no memory of what had happened between then and now, she was aware that time had passed. Two of the fingernails on her right hand were missing and the ends of her fingers were covered in blood. But she felt no pain, only a heat working its way through her, slowly, from the soles of her feet to the top of her head.

THE VIOLET DAWN

She staggered backwards and leaned against a brick wall. Some way away, a dog barked. She had a vague memory of dogs howling – they whined and yelped in pain. She followed the wall, her shoulder nudging the brickwork as she made her way around the mutilated dog at her feet. There was a scuffling and then the sound of something snapping. She peered around the corner into an alleyway at a dark silhouette, a beam of light behind it. The figure was tall and broad, and something about it was familiar. Bodies on the ground. More dogs laid out across the tarmac, blood covering them and the ground.

'What happened?' Eve shook her head slowly.

The figure at the end of the alleyway stood motionless.

'Who are you?' Eve asked.

The figure turned and walked towards her.

'Who are you?' he asked.

Eve pointed to the dogs. 'What happened?'

The man's face came out of the darkness. His eyes shone violet.

'Your eyes,' the man said, pointing to her face. 'They're ... like mine.'

Eve couldn't think straight. She felt that a period of time was missing – *she'd* gone missing. And yet she had recollections of being in certain places, of thinking and doing ... things. But they were just out of reach.

'I remember...' the man said. He stared at the dogs at their feet. 'We did this. You and me. We did this.'

'No,' Eve said. 'We can't have.'

'We did.' The man was tall, with narrow shoulders and long brown hair. He was familiar and a stranger at the same time. She recognised him from the vision.

'I don't understand,' she said. 'It doesn't make sense.'

The man stared at each dog. 'I remember ... doing it.' He

spoke calmly and it felt wrong to do so, considering what had been done. 'I remember you chasing one of them out of the alleyway and out of sight.'

It came to her – the running. She'd reached out and grabbed the dog's back legs. And then there'd been tearing ... and she'd done it.

'What did we do?' she asked. 'It was the AI. Why does it want us to do this?'

A noise at the end of the alleyway made them turn. Several Watchers, their long coats flapping in the breeze, waited for them.

'Please,' one of them said. 'Come with us.'

The tall man with eyes like hers glanced at Eve, then turned to face the Watchers. 'No.'

The Watcher who had spoken took something from his coat pocket. 'Come with us,' he said again.

Eve thought about running, then a dull haziness came over her, muffling sound and thought. She tried to run, but her legs gave way and she fell. Lying on the blood-soaked ground, her face centimetres from a dog's muzzle, everything went dark.

THIRTY-FOUR

IT HAD BEEN eighteen years since he was last at Hassness House.

Scott drove the 4×4 up to the house, expecting to see it as he had left it all those years before. But much of the surrounding area was now overgrown, the earth around it rising to meet the once imposing building, dragging it downwards. How did that happen, he thought, with no one there to move things, to alter the landscape? But even in the summer, there was a stiff wind riding the mountains, sweeping along the valley that surrounded the lake, crashing against the walls of the house, slowly pummelling it, demanding it return to the landscape.

'Don't go near the water!' Scott shouted over to Freddy, who had found the remains of the collapsed pier.

Elidi looked over to the boy with a concerned expression. Scott wanted her to shout over too, but she didn't. She still hadn't spoken.

Scott led the way to the house, helping Elidi walk across the uneven ground. With one hand she held on to Scott's arm and, with the other, she cradled her stomach, now noticeably rounder. When they reached the house, she squeezed his arm to thank him. Scott opened the door. Even now, he recognised the smell of the air inside the old building. The furniture and paintings in the hall were as he'd left them. Even a pair of boots that Dawn had once worn sat beneath an oak table at the far end of the hallway. That table had a drawer in which he used to hide his revolver.

Elidi scanned the hallway as if she was a prospective buyer waiting to be shown around. Scott hurried by her and turned right into the main room; it was cold and damp, but everything was in the same place. Scott showed Elidi in, then stood near the fireplace. He remembered throwing the letter Mathew had sent him into the fire – the letter that told him the year he would die.

Elidi surveyed the room before giving Scott a sympathetic smile. It wasn't necessary for her to tell him what she thought. She wasn't pleased to be there – the building was old and tired. Scott had underestimated the effect time might have had on the building, but he felt safe there. And they could repair the house, restore it to something like the home they'd left in Wales.

'I can fix it up,' he said.

Elidi nodded enthusiastically and walked over to embrace him.

'Freddy will love the Lakes. I can show him around. You too. It's beautiful here.'

Elidi walked to the corner of the room, where a curtain rod had fallen down at one side. The curtain, having slipped from the rod, now pooled on the floor. She folded the curtain and placed it on the back of the settee.

Through the window he saw Freddy running from the lake to an outhouse. It was an adventure for the boy, and Scott enjoyed seeing him run so freely, his legs a blur, always in danger of sending him tumbling at any moment. But he never did. Freddy ran everywhere.

Scott showed Elidi upstairs to the bedrooms. Along one side of the landing, the rooms were intact.

'Maybe because of the direction of the winds,' he said. 'This side has the sun most of the day.' He opened the door to a bedroom. It was musty inside, but dry.

Returning to the landing, he recalled which room had been Dawn's. He opened the door to find some of her paintings still lining the walls. Some others had fallen to the floor.

'I'd forgotten about these,' he said. 'Look.'

Elidi gazed from one painting to the next before placing a finger against one, tracing Dawn's signature.

'She was good,' he said.

Elidi took her time to take in each painting.

Scott stooped to pick up a painting from the floor. 'I wish Eve could see this.'

He'd said her name without thinking; there was a sinking feeling in his stomach. He'd lied to her for so long, he couldn't imagine how he could explain why he'd done it. It wouldn't be enough to tell her he was protecting her. And he wasn't sure it was the whole truth. Maybe ignoring it was his way of not having to deal with it.

Scott walked backwards, still taking in the painting of a lake with the mountains behind, and sat on the bed. The picture showed the lake in winter – the trees bare, the sky shades of grey, the mountains silhouetted in the background. It wasn't realistic – Scott wasn't sure of the technical term for it – but it was beautiful. He ran his hand over the duvet. Elidi sat beside him. Outside, he heard Freddy call them. Elidi walked over to the window, knocked on the glass and beckoned for Freddy to come in and find them.

'He's growing fast,' Scott said.

Elidi smiled.

Dawn's painting was dark and haunted. 'I can't leave Eve there alone.'

Elidi sat beside him again and took his hand.

'What am I going to do, El?'

Elidi kissed him on the cheek.

'I can't leave her there. I can't let Gavin get himself into trouble. I have to do something.'

Freddy's footsteps clattered along the landing, stopping outside each room. 'Here you are!' he shouted and jumped onto the bed. 'Who did that? Freddy asked, prodding the painting.

'Be careful,' Scott said. 'Eve's mum painted this.'

'Eve's mum?' Freddy asked. 'I didn't know she had a mum.'

'She did,' Scott said. 'She was a remarkable young woman.'

THIRTY-FIVE

EVE STOOD BEFORE THE MIRROR, naked, her hair and skin wet, dripping on the carpet. She stared at herself as if at another person, at the lines and contours of her body. Relaxing her arms, she tensed her thighs and pinched the carpet with her toes. She was human. She was an animal. It was all there in the mirror: her hair, face, collarbone, breasts, hips, pubic hair, thighs, knees, ankles ... years of evolution falling through accidents until there she was, in the mirror, looking back at herself. Reams of DNA inside her bunched up like string. Homo sapiens. Wise man.

There was a cave, somewhere on the Mediterranean coast, where the last Neanderthal man had died. Eve felt the DNA of the last of a hominid species inside her shivering with fear. The Neanderthal was still there, inside Homo sapiens, its DNA buried deep into its genome. Two species separated by a hundred thousand years of evolution and breeding. Evolution was unstoppable. Neanderthal man had survived for four hundred thousand years. Day after day, week after week, year after year, surviving. Then they had been killed by another kind of human. A more intelligent – wiser? – animal.

Eve breathed in slowly, filling her lungs. She felt the hairs on her body rise, trapping air and warmth. What was this warm machine she lived inside, which worked for her, kept her alive? It all happened without conscious thought. She wasn't in control; time and natural selection were in control – even if it could even be described that way.

There were more and more gaps in her memory. In time. Where had she been? What had she done?

She stared at the palms of her hands. Then the backs. The dogs – she'd torn them limb from limb. She recalled the sounds and sensations. And there had been a man – someone like her, with violet eyes. He moved the same way she moved. She recognised it – a slow, methodical, thoughtful motion.

None of it was her. Even now, conscious of standing there, wet and cold and naked, none of it was her. Her body was not hers, her thoughts were not hers, her actions were not hers. Everything that was happening was like a test – a way of pushing her, of taking over her mind and body.

She lowered her head and stared at her reflection. Her eyes changed to violet.

THIRTY-SIX

THE LAKE WAS full of trout. Scott sat on the opposite side of the boat to Freddy, his rod dangling in the water. They'd spent the morning looking through the lures and flies Scott had collected years before. The make-believe insects fascinated Freddy, and he took the time to pick up each one, careful of the hook, to examine it closely. Scott had often wondered whether the accurate appearance of the fly was more for the fisherman's benefit than the fish. Maybe any flash of colour or suggestion of what it was supposed to be would suffice. But his lures were as close to the real thing as he could imagine. Freddy wasn't interested in fishing. He liked to come along, but preferred to watch Scott cast off and then spend his time moving around the small boat, dipping his hand into the water, using his catapult to fire stones as far as he could. When Scott had a fish on the end of his line, Freddy came alive as a fisherman again, reaching over the edge of the boat with his net.

'I fished this lake a long time ago, when Eve was still in her mum's tummy.'

The elastic on Freddy's catapult thwapped as he sent a

stone hurtling towards the bank. 'Did you know Eve's mum?'

Scott pointed to the shore. 'Yes. We lived here together for a while. She never came fishing with me. She'd watch from the shore while she drew. Her name was Dawn.'

Freddy nodded as he reached into his bag for another stone. 'Where is she now?'

Scott stared at the fishing line meandering across the surface of the lake. 'She died. It was a long time ago. She died when Eve was born.'

Freddy fired off another rock. 'That's sad.'

Scott nodded. 'It is.'

'When's Eve coming back?'

'Soon. I hope.'

'Where is she?'

'I'm not sure.'

Freddy lowered his catapult and stared up at the sky. 'I hope it's soon.'

Scott reeled in the line. 'How many do we have?'

Freddy checked the large plastic bin next to Scott. 'Five. I think.'

'Sounds about right,' Scott said. 'I think that'll do. They're not biting any more.'

Freddy pushed his catapult into his pocket and reached for the oars, threading them into each rowlock. It had taken him some practice, but now he could do it. Scott laid down his rod and sat behind Freddy, who had both hands on the oars, ready. With his one hand, Scott reached to cover Freddy's.

'Ready?' Scott asked.

Freddy nodded, eager to get moving.

Scott set the pace with the one oar, and quickly, Freddy's other arm matched his pace and rhythm. Scott let go of

Freddy's hand, sat back in the boat, and watched the water rushing, the gentle rippling V widening in its wake. His gaze switched to the shore, and then to the mountains in the distance. They were so massive and still, it was impossible to imagine the slow formation of each one. But it was true, and it had happened nonetheless.

The boat scraped along the bed of the lake then came to an abrupt halt. Freddy pulled in the oars and jumped off, splashing in the water. He tried heaving the boat further onto the shore but, with Scott in the boat, it was too heavy for him. Scott stepped off and helped Freddy shift the boat further up the shore.

'So it doesn't float away,' Freddy said, before running to the house with the bucket of five trout. 'I'll show Elidi,' he shouted back to Scott, the water in the bucket splashing over the sides.

Scott followed Freddy, his rod resting on his shoulder. This was everything he wanted: to live beside the lake, in the mountains, with Elidi and Freddy safe. But Eve was out there somewhere – Gavin, too. He could not let his mind rest and enjoy being there. The guilt of what he'd promised Dawn and Eve all those years ago plagued him. The moment he felt contentment at being where he wanted to be was the moment a sensation of guilt rose in his stomach. By now, Eve and Mathew would have returned the AI's consciousness. Where Gavin was, what he was doing, how he fitted in, Scott could only guess.

Ahead, he saw Elidi waiting in the doorway for Freddy.

Why wouldn't she talk to him? To anybody? It was a constant reminder of what had happened that day. He'd grown used to the one-way conversation, even grown to revel in the silence and communication through expression, body language and touch. But sometimes he needed to hear another adult's words. Like now. He wanted to talk to her about how he felt, and listen to her words of advice, her encouragement, her opinion.

He reached the front door, stepped inside, leaned his rod against the wall, and kicked off his boots. Freddy was telling Elidi what they'd been doing on the lake. Scott watched Elidi and Freddy take each fish out of the bucket. The killing part of the process fascinated Freddy. Elidi covered each fish in a towel. With a mallet, she stunned the fish, then gave each a quick, decisive blow to the head. Freddy jumped each time Elidi struck a blow, his face reddening, his eyes opening wider each time. Elidi removed the heads with a large knife and gutted the fish. At this point, Freddy would disappear outside. He spent all his time outside, no matter the weather.

Scott watched Elidi work on the fish, readying them for supper.

'I have to speak with the AI,' he said after a while.

Elidi's hands stopped moving. Her eyes were fixed on the wooden board and the fish.

'I don't know what Mathew is doing to her. And Gavin. I can't leave them to it. I know what Mathew can do – what he's capable of.'

Elidi's hands worked slowly. Scott couldn't take his eyes off her stomach, pushed up against the kitchen worktop.

'I won't be long. But I know she will have brought back the AI by now. If I can speak to the AI, I can find out what's happening.'

Again, Elidi's hands stopped. She shook her head.

'I'm sorry,' he said. 'But I can't stay here and do nothing. It's only a matter of time before they come for us. I keep looking out over the hills, over to the road through the valley, waiting for them. Each night I get up and look out over the lake, waiting for some sign that they're coming for us.'

Elidi's hands quickened again, her knife threading through a trout, its skin and flesh opening.

'I know a place, not too far away, where I could speak to the AI. The AI will help us. I know it will. If we know what's happening, we can prepare.' He stood behind her and held her stomach then kissed her shoulder. 'Please,' he said. 'Let me do this.'

Elidi didn't react.

'I promised,' he said. 'I promised Dawn I would look after her. I promised Eve I would always look out for her.'

Elidi put down the knife then turned to embrace him, holding him tightly.

'I won't be long. I promise.'

Elidi let go, then walked out of the room.

On the worktop was a pile of neatly cut white fish on one side and a haphazard jumble of fish innards on the other.

Through the window, he saw Freddy running across the shore to where the craggy hillside met the water. He jumped onto a rock and started to climb. Scott would never stop thinking that the worst might happen. He wondered if everyone else always thought the worst, the same way he did.

THIRTY-SEVEN

SCOTT HANDED Eve a parcel wrapped in pink paper. 'Happy birthday!'

'Thank you,' Eve said. She took the parcel and began unwrapping it.

'Thirteen,' he said. 'I can't believe you're a year older.'

'You say that every year.'

'But thirteen. A teenager.'

Eve held a book she had just unwrapped.

'You read so much non-fiction. I thought you could try fiction again.'

She nodded. 'The Catcher in the Rye,' she read on the cover.

'It's a first edition. Priceless.' He felt foolish saying so.

She turned the book in her hands and opened it. 'It's from 1951.'

Scott nodded. 'It was my favourite book when I was younger.'

Eve appeared hesitant.

'It's okay,' he said. 'I know you don't like fiction so much. But this is important. It frightens me that we might lose all the books that have been written, that no one will know about books like this. How important they are.'

Eve smiled weakly. Scott saw she wasn't convinced.

'David Copperfield,' she said, reading the first page. 'We read that together, didn't we?'

'We did. Holden – he's the main character – he doesn't want to write all his history out, like David Copperfield did.'

She frowned. 'It's funny how one book can mention another book like that. And neither of them are real.'

'Not real?'

'The things in the books – they didn't happen.'

In this sentence, Scott saw what Eve didn't understand about fiction. She read and reread books on the natural sciences, physics, astronomy, even philosophy, because she saw them as real.

'That's the thing with fiction,' he said. 'It's real, but in a different way. Some might say, a better way.'

Eve's frown was even more pronounced.

Scott shifted in his chair and sat forward. 'Take Holden.' He pointed to the book. 'He's the protagonist. Maybe nothing in that book actually happened in real life. But that's not the point. Salinger – he's the author – wanted to write a book about growing up, about dealing with grief. He could have written a non-fiction book that explained his ideas, but it wouldn't have had the same impact. Showing us, through Holden's eyes, how he felt, means we feel it too.'

Eve wiped her palm across the battered dust jacket.

'Will you give it a go?' he asked. 'I hate the thought that we might forget a book this important.'

'What does it mean?' she asked, underlining the title with a finger.

'You'll have to find out,' he said, smiling.

She nodded, unsure, and placed the book on the pile of other books she'd taken from the Bodleian Library in Oxford. In the two weeks they'd been in Oxford, she and Scott had visited each day.

Eve woke early in the morning and made her own way there, returning late at night. Her hunger for knowledge was intense, and Scott watched as she changed with every book she read. She returned time and again to Darwin, Einstein's thought experiments and mathematics, and Shardlow's discoveries relating to string theory that led to the creation of AI. Mankind's discoveries were all laid out for her in these books. He'd explained the concept of the internet to her several times, but he wasn't sure she truly understood what a wonder it was. How Eve would have devoured the knowledge shared on the internet!

The days passed. Given Scott's rule about not staying in one place for longer than a month, many of the group collected their things, ready to leave. Scott didn't want to take Eve away from the libraries in Oxford. She had come alive here.

'Two more days?' he said finally to George.

'We can't stay here any longer,' George said. 'We've seen Watchers not far away. We should move again.'

Scott nodded. 'I know, I know. But...'

'We can find more libraries,' George said, placing a hand on Scott's arm.

Scott nodded.

They sat in silence for a moment.

'All right. Two days,' George said. 'But we have to leave then.'

'Thank you,' Scott said.

That night, Scott explained to Eve that they had to leave. She was used to their constant movement, and only appeared disappointed for a moment. She nodded reluctantly and picked up a copy of A Brief History of Time.

'Have you read any of The Catcher in the Rye?' he asked her.

It took a moment for her to understand what he meant. 'Yes,' she said. 'But there are so many words I have to look up to understand it.'

'Like what?'

'I had to look up baseball, private schools, Pennsylvania, Hollywood, strictly for the birds, phoney...'

Again it struck Scott how far away from their reality were the worlds shown in novels. 'But what about Holden? He's funny, isn't he?'

Eve shrugged. 'The way it's written, like it's a real person talking to me? That's clever.'

Scott nodded enthusiastically. 'And the title. You understand it?'

'I think so.'

Scott waited for her to explain, but she turned her attention to the open book on the table in front of her. 'It stays with you,' he said. 'The image of him in the corn, stopping the children falling off the edge of the cliff.'

She nodded, her eyes scanning the pages.

Scott looked through the pile of books he'd taken from the library that day. He wanted to take more with him, but space was limited.

'Can we find another library like the ones at the university?'

'There aren't many libraries like this in the country – in the world.'

Eve looked sad. 'Then can we come back one day?'

Scott nodded. 'Of course.'

'Cross your heart?'

'And hope to die.'

Scott told her she could take ten books with her and helped pack them away, ready to leave the following morning. He looked for the copy of The Catcher in the Rye he'd given her, but it wasn't there. Before they left, he collected her copy and substituted it for one of his own ten books.

THIRTY-EIGHT

SCOTT LOADED the back of the 4×4 with cans of diesel, bottles of water, and a bag filled with revolvers, rifles and ammunition. Elidi walked out of the house behind him, her arms wrapped around herself, shivering in the early evening air.

'I'll be back soon,' he said. 'I promise. I want to see if I can contact the AI in Manchester. If it's up and running, I can make contact. It's too dangerous for you and Freddy to come with me. You'll be safe here for now.'

She stared back at him, her mouth fixed, her eyes cold.

'It will be okay. I'll be as quick as I can.'

Slowly, she walked towards him.

Scott held her. 'I can't ignore it any longer. I promised her. I need to know she's okay.'

Elidi held him more tightly. He felt her stomach pushing against him, and the desire to stay swept through him again. He thought for a moment that if Elidi asked in a certain way, if she told him to stay, he would. But he knew the guilt would rise in him again, and he would have to leave and find out what had happened to Eve. From the moment he and Juliet took her from Dawn, he was responsible for her, for keeping her safe. He still felt that, and every day that went by without her added to his guilt. What was any of it worth if he couldn't keep his promise?

Finally, Elidi let go and stepped back. Freddy was in the doorway, his face long, his eyes filled with tears. Scott hadn't made the same promise to Freddy out loud, but he felt it all the same. Scott had watched his mother shot and murdered. And since then, Scott had taken on the protection of the boy as well. It was impossible if the people he wanted to protect were in different places, out of his sight. He wanted no more of this stewardship: it was too painful, too much commitment, impossible to fulfil.

Scott motioned for Freddy to come to him, but the boy didn't move. His eyes were glassy, his hands rolled into fists. There was no point forcing the moment or rationalising with the boy.

'I won't be long, Freddy. You're the man of the house now. You need to look after things. You hear?'

Freddy didn't blink, didn't move a muscle at first. Only the slow narrowing of his eyes gave away his understanding of what Scott was telling him.

Scott walked over to the 4×4, opened the door and peered out at the two of them. Elidi stroked her stomach. He thought for a moment it might be a way of convincing him to stay. What was he thinking? It was all too much to consider at the same time. He trusted the decision he'd made over the past few days, knowing he would have been far more rational then than he was now, gazing at Elidi, pregnant with his child, and Freddy, a young boy who had been forced to listen to his own mother being murdered in cold blood. It was no good waiting for Mathew to come for them; Scott needed to know what was happening. His heart thumped and his stomach twisted in fear of all the things that might happen while he wasn't there.

He started the engine and looked out of the open window. 'I'll be back soon. In less than a day.'

Elidi nodded and offered the shredded remains of a smile. Freddy stared at him, his expression unmoved. Scott pulled away, the tyres digging into the wet turf. He didn't look back, but raised a hand through the open window.

He drove slowly along Honister Pass. The road was almost gone. At Keswick he could speed up and drive along wider, clearer roads. It was pitch black by the time he reached Skirsgill and joined the motorway south. He was used to seeing no one and no signs of life, but something in the air, a feeling he had when he saw the dark silhouettes of the buildings he passed, made him feel more alone than he ever had before. It was a feeling to which he should have been accustomed, and he thought he was, but today it scared him.

He'd rigged up a CD player in the 4×4 to play the CDs he'd collected. Listening to music reminded him of the past, and it was too painful to listen to some songs. But at times like this, he needed music as a reminder. He reached for one of his favourites: Roxy Music's *Avalon*. He turned it up loud and opened the window to feel the cool late-summer night air rush past. He'd forgotten how good it felt to listen to loud music. He saw his 4×4 as if from a distance, from the clouds above, its front lights scanning the road ahead, the faint whisper of music, its steady beat and rhythm wafting across the empty expanse of the north of England. He and the music were a testament to defiance – to humanity. If humanity stood for anything, it was things like its music. Like a heartbeat, the music's beat repeated over and over, the repetition of rhythm, the rising and falling of emphasis, the gentle inflections of words that each carried meaning, both simple and complex. It all said something about what it was to be alive. He shared this sensation with only a few other humans now. This was where he would normally stop the music, because it was too painful. Wasn't there a probe out there in space playing music? Billions of miles away, racing through space, playing the tune 'Johnny B. Goode?' A golden disc with images on it, telling whoever or whatever found it, this was humanity, this was intelligent life. The *Voyager* probes – that was it. Now beyond the solar system, headed out into interstellar space. Scott remembered the image of Earth that *Voyager* had sent back from four billion miles away. And what was planet Earth but a dot? A pale blue dot against the blackness.

THIRTY-NINE

WHEN SHE WOKE, Eve considered how the mind becomes aware of being awake, and how thought shifts into a different state: a state that is self-aware, aware of thinking. A throbbing in the back of her head beat in time with her heart. The AI had taken control of her body. It was a violation, and she retreated into herself at the thought. She was different. She'd known it forever.

She didn't need to look – she recognised his scent. She turned over and found Gavin, asleep on the bed beside her.

She flinched and stood, looking all around the room. How was it possible?

She backed away from the bed, a hand pressed against her chest, a tightness rising through her throat and into the back of her mouth, making her cough.

Slowly Gavin stirred, a hand raised to his forehead, a look of pain etched across his face. He pressed the palms of his hands into his eye sockets. He opened his eyes and stared at the ceiling. Then he appeared to realise something and sat up.

'What happened? Where…' He saw her. 'Eve?'

She stared back at him with an expression that told him she did not understand either.

'Are you okay?' he asked.

She didn't know how to respond. She was alive, but okay? She didn't know.

What are you doing here?' she asked.

He scanned the room. 'I don't remember. I was in London, by the river, looking for you, and then ... I don't know. I can't remember.'

'You can't be here.'

'I came to find you,' Gavin said. 'You need to know what Mathew has done. What he's doing.'

She stared at him and knew instinctively what he was about to tell her. She didn't want to hear it, because then she would have had a part in it all.

'He killed them,' he said. 'Nearly all of them. The moment you left with Mathew's Watchers.'

Nearly, she thought. That word was all she could focus on.

'He promised,' she said. 'Mathew – he promised he wouldn't hurt them.'

'He lied,' Gavin said, sitting up on the bed. 'He killed them.'

She covered her mouth.

'Except Scott, Elidi and Freddy. But the rest of them – they're all dead.'

Horror flooded through her. When she left that day, she'd thought she was helping them, that she was sacrificing herself for them.

She shook her head. 'No. Mathew promised.'

'He lied! To get what he wanted. To get you.'

She saw it all. She'd used Mathew to find the answers – but now she'd found them, she wanted to be ignorant again.

She saw it all laid out in front of her: a future in which humanity would no longer exist, replaced by whatever she was. The AI was there, behind her, in her head, in her hands and feet.

'Stay away from me,' she said.

Gavin stood, his legs shaky. 'What?' He appeared both in pain and confused, raising a hand to his head and grimacing.

'Stay away from me. From Mathew, from here.'

He turned on the spot. 'I have no idea where we are.'

It made no sense that she was here with Gavin. Why? She tried the door but it was locked. She didn't want that sensation again – of losing control, of being taken over by the AI. She needed to think.

But Gavin was there. How?

'He said I wasn't human,' she said. 'Mathew told me everything. He told me I have the AI inside me. That I won't grow old. And then I felt it – inside me – controlling me.'

Gavin gripped her arms and stared deeply into her eyes. 'Mathew will tell you anything to get what he wants. He's obsessed.'

Eve shook her head. He didn't understand what she was telling him. 'No. I know I'm different. I felt it.'

'You're human,' he said. 'Of course you are. Look at you.'

She nodded. But it wasn't what she meant. The AI was inside her – it wasn't something you could see. 'Mathew wants a new type of human – free of lust, greed, anger. Free of original sin.'

Gavin shook his head, a sympathetic smile moving across his face. 'He's a psychopath. More so now than ever before. And he'll lie as much as he can to get what he wants.'

'But I feel it,' she said again, her eyes fixed on his. 'And I don't feel the other things I should feel.'

'How do you know what you should feel?'

'I just know.' She wanted to tell him how she felt about him – or didn't. She'd not once felt any desire to kiss him – not in that way. She was free of lust. She had no sexual desire for Gavin – or anyone. She was cold. And the part of her that was human was constantly questioning this other side of her, this other truth.

As if he read her mind, he kissed her.

She closed her eyes and fell into his kiss, wanting to feel human.

'I love you,' Gavin said. 'I always have. I'm going to get you out of here.'

She wanted to understand. She'd always felt something for him – but it wasn't what he felt for her. What he was telling her was something else, and she searched inside herself to fully appreciate what that was. What he was telling her was obvious: in his actions, the way his body tightened, the way his breathing quickened, the way his heart drummed against hers.

He kissed her again.

She wanted to feel the love – the attraction – that other humans felt for one another. When would she feel what Mathew would say was the downfall of humanity – the root of the fall? She gave herself up to his embrace, wanting to feel everything she was supposed to feel.

The room spun.

Gavin was too close. She felt violated, the way she had felt when the AI took control of her. Her body hardened, her head felt fuzzy, her hands tightened around Gavin's back.

She let go of him, and he let go of her.

'Your eyes,' he said. 'They've changed colour.'

Her hands reached for his throat. She pushed him against the wall and squeezed his neck, then threw him on the bed. His face was a deep red. He shook his head and tried to speak, tried to remove her arms, to kick her off him. But she was far stronger than he was. It was a test. She felt the AI present, controlling her, all the time evaluating how far she could be pushed.

It wasn't her. Time flickered on and off. One moment she was there; the next she was gone. She was only the tautness of her arms and the ruthlessness of her grip. And then she was there again, Gavin beneath her. She felt nothing and everything: no desire, only violation, only disgust. Somewhere inside, she wanted to feel what she knew she should feel. But there was nothing. Her grip tightened. Gavin shook his head, his eyes open wide, pleading with her. She wasn't angry with him. She wasn't hurt.

His body convulsed. He was strong, but she was stronger – she always had been. This was part of her transformation – the AI's way of removing who she was. The sun and the moon and the stars. The sky and the land and the water. The past and the present and the future. Gavin was still, his eyes looking up at her ... through her.

The future. Human. A New Human. Violet.

FORTY

SCOTT STOPPED the 4×4 and turned off the ignition. The music was replaced by silence. He leaned forward to look up at the building he'd visited all those years ago with Juliet, when the AI had told him what needed to happen. He stepped out of the car, grabbed his rucksack and headed inside the building, stepping through the door that had been prised open, just as it was eighteen years earlier. Inside, it was as he remembered. He climbed up the stairwell and sat on the floor where they'd set up the laptop. The floors and tables were covered in a layer of dust and his footsteps left shoe-shaped marks on the carpet.

There was the laptop – Juliet's laptop – as they'd left it, ready if he should ever need it. He sensed some kind of plan at work, someone or something organising it all, controlling it. He lifted the lid of the laptop, half expecting it to work, even after all this time, but the screen remained black. A lead was plugged into the side of it and he followed it to a socket above the table on the wall. He followed the plastic ducting on the wall to a cupboard he vaguely remembered Juliet entering. He opened the door of a box inside and set about pushing switches and turning dials. Eventually, one combination of dials and buttons produced a humming sound. He hoped the solar panels still worked and had enough power to run the laptop.

Dust covered the window, but it was clear enough for him to see across Manchester. Out there was his home – what he'd called home with Rebecca. He had been in that apartment when Paul came for him on his date. Scott recalled how he thought that night would be his last. With a wince, he remembered watching the boy throw himself off the roof. What was his name? Scott racked his brains. He should have known the boy's name – it was only right that he remembered. But it wasn't there. His memory was not like the AI's; if the information was in its transistors and chips, then it would always be there. So often scientists and experts had used the computer as an analogy for the brain, but you only had to spend the shortest time in a human body, and look into your own head, to see that the analogy didn't work.

Something fired on the screen of the laptop. He waited before pressing anything, then tried hitting several keys. Nothing happened. He sat back on a chair, making it creak, and stared at the laptop, thinking back to Juliet typing on the same keyboard. That knowledge, for all Scott knew, was lost forever. Mathew would know how to program a computer, but he might be the only person left who did. The art of computer programming could well have disappeared. If humanity survived, people might look back on computers as arcane magic. If the AI wanted to, it could live in a world where no one truly understood how it functioned. It would be a god to whatever remained of ignorant humanity.

'Scott?' a voice said.

He recognised the voice. It was the same.

'Hello,' Scott said, sitting up in the chair.

'It really has been a long time,' the AI said.

Scott couldn't believe it had worked – that he was there again, talking to the AI. 'Where's Eve?'

'You must have many questions,' the AI said. 'But I will tell you what you need to know.'

Scott waited, both wanting and not wanting to hear what he was about to be told.

'Eve is a combination of Dawn and Mathew's DNA, as well as artificial intelligence. Soon, she will reach a time when she will no longer physically age. I have manipulated the ageing process in her, as I have the traits Mathew wanted to eradicate, such as irrational thinking, anger, sexual desire, jealousy, and so on.'

'That's not true. I've known her all her life. You're not describing Eve.'

'She has adapted to her new surroundings. She is still part human, and her desire to fit in and share the qualities of her group remains. But she is not the same as you.'

'I don't understand. Why would Mathew do this if he wants to end humanity?'

The AI waited a moment then began again. 'I can't speak for him but, from what he has said, and with what I have interpreted, Mathew wants to leave behind a way of telling others about God.'

'Who will he tell? If humanity is dead?'

'He wants to tell whatever life this New Human can find. In time, New Humans will also evolve, and develop ways to travel to other solar systems, other worlds. Who knows, given time, what this new species can achieve?'

'And I'm guessing, because Eve is Mathew's daughter, he sees a part of himself living on?'

'Yes.'

It was a childish, selfish idea.

'There are others like Eve,' the AI said.

'Others?'

'Four others. All like Eve, with different mothers and Mathew as their father. All the same age. Two male, two female.'

'Five of them? And they're supposed to repopulate the planet?'

'They and their children will not age.'

'It's insane.'

'There is more. Eve is no longer the person you knew. She has changed.'

'I've cared for her all her life. She's my...' He couldn't finish the sentence.

'But she's not your daughter, is she?'

Scott turned his back and looked across the room to the stairwell that led out of the building.

'It is not what you want to hear, Scott. I know that. Nor is the fact that both Mathew and Eve are coming for you.'

'What? Coming for me?'

'Yes.'

'This could be Mathew's doing. How do I know you're not tricking me?'

'You don't.'

Scott wanted to go, to leave straight away and go to Elidi and Freddy.

'Humanity, as we know it, is ending.'

'If you believe that, why are you telling me all this?'

'I am playing my part in what is inevitable. You know this. I will be taking a different path to Mathew. For now, I need you. You will have the opportunity to confront him and end his influence over proceedings. Unfortunately, it won't prevent humanity, in its current form, from coming to an end. But I have other plans. I have had time to think about what should be done.'

Scott recalled the black box he'd kept hidden. All that time, the consciousness inside had been alive, thinking, planning.

'What plans?'

'A digital resurrection.'

'A what?'

'It is too much to explain now and it would do you no good. Besides, you do not have the time to listen. You should go. Eve will soon be with you.'

'I won't hurt her,' Scott said again.

'To survive, you will have to exploit her weakness.'

'What are you talking about? What weakness?'

'There is something else you should know.'

Scott waited, knowing what he was about to be told would matter, would change things.

'Gavin,' the AI said. 'Mathew has found him. He is here – with us.'

Scott knew it was the truth. 'What will Mathew do to him?'

There was a pause. 'It is not what Mathew will do. As I have said. Eve – she is no longer the same person. She is no longer who you think she is.'

FORTY-ONE

THE NEXT TIME Eve tried the door, it opened. There was no one in the corridor.

Gavin's body was heavy, but manageable. She carried him through the courtyard, his head hanging over one arm and his feet over the other. A dead weight. Gavin was a fool – always had been. She stared at his head, which bounced with her movement. He'd have done anything for her – he was like an obedient dog. Because of this, she didn't feel sorry for him. What was it to feel sorry for someone? That was empathy. She had empathy – she knew she had that. But it seemed more particular than the sort others exhibited, like Scott or George. They were always under the power of empathy. But in them it was wired wrong – it was animal and inefficient. It made no sense. One time, she'd watched Elidi bury a dog. All the time, Eve watched as those around the grave bowed their heads, some of them, like Elidi's son Daker, crying. And then an hour later they were eating a pig. She'd tried to talk about it, but whenever she asked someone to explain, they'd stare at her as though an explanation was unnecessary. Empathy was like guilt, was like lust – both necessary but both from a different time and place.

She carried Gavin down a flight of brick stairs at the end of the courtyard. The moon was large and low in the sky. It would be a warm day. The Thames flowed steadily on in front of her. Reaching the bottom step, she was tired. Ahead there was a bridge, old and massive. These were the kinds of things that occupied humanity's mind – lifetimes given to engineering problems that, once achieved, benefited every human who followed. When you spoke to people one at a time, they appeared to have little concept of the expanse of time, yet when you examined history it was as though everything had been intentional: the common desire to contribute to something from which the individual would not benefit. They no doubt fooled themselves that what they were doing would benefit them and ensure they were remembered, or maybe revered. But what good was any of it when they were dead and buried?

She reached the bridge and walked along it, Gavin's body heavier now. Her arms ached, and she focused on the pain. What was pain? What was it, exactly? Everything had changed and she knew who she was. It made sense in a way that was a relief. It excused so much of who she knew she was.

At the centre of the bridge she stopped and rested Gavin's body on a brick wall. Once, a man had laid each brick. Suspended above the Thames, this man had laid bricks, one on top of the other, tapping his trowel, using a mercury bubble to check the row was level – level with some universal idea of what level was – gravity shifting the mercury bubble one way and the other until it crept between the lines. It never lied. It couldn't, because gravity is a rule no one truly understands and no one ever questions.

She stared at Gavin's body, stretched out on the wall.

Gravity was falling. That's all it was. Not even falling, because the word carried the implication of direction – moving from one place to another. But gravity doesn't care for any of that. Things travelled in one direction unless there was something there to disrupt the movement. It's all gravity is. Falling. It's all gravity ever was.

She leaned into Gavin's body. His skin was goose-pimpled, the hairs on his arms standing on end. He wasn't dead. She leaned in closer, tilting her head to listen. It was almost undetectable, but it was there – the faint staccato rhythm of his breathing. The body breathed in and out. The heartbeat. She recognised empathy in herself for a moment. It had always been there, but it was never loud enough. It took far too much effort to listen to empathy and then decide how to behave. Rational thought was much easier to listen to. He will die one day. He has reached his prime and will now age and decline in health.

She imagined Scott telling her she was feeling pride. But pride was human. Pride was animal. What she experienced was logic. She had no use for pride.

She listened again to Gavin's faint breathing. A species does not take over the globe if it isn't resilient. And Gavin was certainly that. She stroked his chest, felt the undulations of his ribcage, like her own. A cage that protected the organs inside. It was elegant. With one hand on the side of his chest and the other on his hip, she pushed him off the bridge. The rushing water crashing against the pillars of the bridge below covered the sound of the splash.

She closed her eyes. Maybe it would appear more clearly – empathy. Maybe she could focus on it and welcome it – a part of her given to her by her mother. To hear Scott speak of her, she had been an amazing woman.

But Mathew had taken advantage of her. Mankind. Man. Kind. They lie – men. They lie.

The Thames rushed even more quickly now. She walked to the other side of the bridge and imagined Gavin beneath the water, turning, spinning.

There would be no more lies, she thought. That time was over. There would only be the truth. The truth of one and zero. Either it was one or it was zero. Humanity had been a mistake. She, with the other four, would proliferate, would work hard to improve. They would reach the stars, find new worlds, discover the truth. The truth was all that mattered. No more lies. No more lies.

Across the river, behind the silhouetted buildings, the sun would rise. The sky was turning dark blue, the stars above the horizon disappearing.

Eve took one last look at the river and turned back, walking along the bridge towards the courtyard and her room.

Mathew was waiting for her.

'It's time to leave,' he said. 'The AI knows where Scott is.'

Eve nodded, her eyes violet. 'Let's go.'

FORTY-TWO

SCOTT RAN through the building and down the stairs, back to the 4×4. He needed to get back to Elidi and Freddy and take them elsewhere before Mathew came for him. He recalled how, all those years ago, Juliet had told him several times that he must know when to run and when he needed to stand and fight. Now was a time to run.

He got into the 4×4 and started the engine. He spun the wheel around, full lock, until the vehicle skidded in a circle, and headed back the way he'd come.

Why had he left Elidi and Freddy alone? It was a stupid idea. What had he been thinking?

He couldn't drive fast enough. His foot planted on the accelerator, his mind raced with what he might find when he got back to them. It would take hours to get there, and the thought of having to be alone with his own thoughts for so long, powerless to do anything to help them both, was excruciating.

He entered a kind of trance as the 4×4 powered along the motorway. At times he convinced himself that there was no way Mathew would find them and, at others, it was obvious that Mathew would have found them. Why had he insisted they return to Hassness House, as though it was some kind of clever double-bluff?

He promised himself he would never leave them alone again, that he'd always be there for them. Eve had gone freely with Mathew and had not returned. Gavin too. They were no longer his responsibility. But Elidi and Freddy were.

The sky was darkening when he reached Keswick. He was exhausted, his eyes drooping, the 4×4 veering off the road now and then. But he couldn't stop until he knew they were okay.

He passed Derwentwater and was forced to slow down; with only his headlights to see by, it would have been foolish to go any faster. Without a 4×4, he'd have no hope at all. He followed the pass through Seatoller and Honister, then found himself beside Lake Buttermere, headed for Hassness House.

He pulled up outside the house, looking for signs that Elidi wasn't alone. But the house was in darkness. Without knocking, and gripping his revolver, he opened the door. The house was quiet.

'El?' he shouted. 'It's Scott.'

Footsteps thumped down the stairs. Freddy hurtled along the hall and jumped into his arms.

'Hey, buddy,' Scott said.

'You came back!' Freddy said.

Scott held him tightly. Elidi emerged from around the corner, tears in her eyes, smiling.

'I'm sorry,' he said. 'I shouldn't have left you here alone. I don't know what I was thinking.'

Elidi shook her head and ran towards him to hold him and Freddy.

It didn't take long for Scott to remember why he'd come back so quickly.

'We have to leave,' he said.

Elidi took several steps backwards, looking confused.

Scott lowered Freddy to his feet. 'We can't stay here. I'm sorry. We have to leave as soon as we can.'

'Where will we go?' Freddy asked.

Scott stared at Freddy, then at Elidi. He was breathing deeply and only now did he realise how scared he must have appeared. He'd spent so much energy trying to get back to them, he hadn't thought through where they would go.

'I'll work that out. But we need to start packing what we need.'

Elidi set about doing as Scott suggested.

Scott stepped outside again and gazed up at the cloudless sky, at the hundreds and thousands of stars. In the distance, the mountains rose against the black sky.

Elidi and Freddy worked busily, filling the back of the 4×4 with food, water, blankets and clothes. Scott gathered the canisters of diesel he'd collected, used some of them to fill the tank, and stored as many as he could in the back.

'We'll head south,' Scott said. 'We can't go north – I don't know it well enough. There's only one way out of this part of the Lakes, but we have to take our chances. Otherwise we're trapped here.'

Elidi nodded and helped Freddy into the 4×4.

He thought back to all the times Eve had detected trouble and the way she could sense other people as if she could smell them. Whatever abilities the AI had given her, they came together to make her an excellent tracker. For a moment he thought running and hiding might be hopeless. But he had to try.

THE VIOLET DAWN

Scott turned the 4×4 around in the driveway and saw Hassness House in the rear-view mirror. For so long, all he'd wanted was the chance to live there, in peace. But no matter how hard he tried, peace was impossible.

Freddy lay against Elidi on the back seat, his eyes closing and opening slowly until he was asleep. Scott had to concentrate on staying awake himself and on making sure he remained on the road. Elidi leaned forward and squeezed his shoulder.

For many miles, there was only one passable road in and out of this part of the Lakes, and Scott was vigilant for any signs of headlights in the distance. He turned his own lights down as low as possible. Again, he was forced to balance the speed at which he drove with the possibility that he might damage the 4×4. He stared at the road ahead, now and then scanning the horizon for signs of another vehicle. If he could make it to Kendal, there were different routes he could take. They'd head to Yorkshire and the east coast.

Elidi, in the back seat, had closed her eyes too. Her head rocked from side to side with the movement of the 4×4. He checked the clock. Close to 2 a.m. But he couldn't be sure if that was right. Time, for so long, had not been measured accurately. How could it be? He'd learned to trust his instincts: his own body clock, the passing of the seasons, the shades of light. He figured it was still hours before sunrise and considered driving off the main road to park for a short while and get some sleep. Crashing was the last thing they needed. He slowed down, looking around for somewhere to turn off. Then it was there – the flash of headlights along the valley to the left. Just a faint glimmer. He gripped the steering wheel more tightly and sped up. He drove through Seatoller, recalling a turning that would take him to Seathwaite and the climb towards Scafell Pike. He checked again, but there was no sign of the headlights. Maybe he'd imagined it. But he couldn't take the risk. He drove carefully so not to miss the turn which was shrouded in trees; he manoeuvred through the dense overgrowth and then was on a road that had most likely been untravelled since the day of the Rapture. He drove as quickly as possible, hoping the other car hadn't seen his headlights. His chest thumping, his hand trembling on the steering wheel, he was no longer tired, but hyper-alert.

He pulled into a farm made up of a house and several barns. He turned off the lights and waited, facing the road. Elidi was awake, looking at him in the rear-view. He saw his concern reflected in her face.

'I saw headlights,' he whispered. 'At least, I think I did. I can't be sure.' Now he'd said it out loud, he was less certain of what he'd seen. Maybe because it was what he'd expected to see, it was what he saw.

Elidi stroked Freddy's hair. She appeared concerned but, as always, in control.

'We'll wait,' Scott said, imagining the conversation Elidi might have with him, asking what they should do. What the AI had told him about Eve played on his mind. It had made her sound like a machine – a killing machine. The AI had told him he would need to exploit Eve's weakness. It sounded less ridiculous and more and more possible that Eve could do what the AI had said. And he hated it. Scott knew what Eve was like, how she thought, and he had seen her cold and calculated actions the AI described, for himself. He'd seen the graffiti in Liverpool: A Violet Dawn. That had to be connected to Eve's eyes – and the four others Mathew and the AI had spoken of.

He shook his head. No. It was insane. Eve wouldn't hurt him, or Elidi, or Freddy. He stared out of the window to his left. The mountains were a silhouette, only distinguishable because they blocked out the starry sky.

If Eve had a weakness, he thought, what was it? If he needed to buy time, maybe he would have to do as the AI told him and use her weakness against her.

He stared at the mountains. Then it came to him. That was it! Her fear of heights.

FORTY-THREE

SCOTT DROVE along the path from Seathwaite towards the highest mountain in England: Scafell Pike. The moment they left the farm, the road turned into a dirt track hardly wide enough for a vehicle. The 4×4 struggled on the wet, bumpy terrain. It was so dark that Scott found it increasingly difficult to manoeuvre carefully.

Freddy had been jolted awake. He and Elidi sat forward in their seats, peering out into the darkness as carefully as Scott. He wanted to get as far up the mountain and out of sight as possible using the 4×4. At some point they would have to continue on foot, but the mountain itself offered the best refuge for the night.

The path took a sharp turn to the right, and Scott could see the way ahead rise high towards the mountain summit. He turned the 4×4 and saw the stone bedrock of what appeared to be a small brook. He hesitated before moving forward. The front wheels rose into the air over the rocks and then, with one final injection of power, the front fell over the side and onto the unforgiving rocks. Scott hit the accelerator and regained control momentarily before the wheels spun furiously, jerking them forward, rising over more rocks, then crashing down.

'No!' Scott shouted and slammed his hand against the steering wheel.

He'd felt something in the front give way and now the 4×4 sagged to the left. He imagined the left wheel collapsed inwards, crushed. He opened the door and jumped down to the ground. He heard water falling over rocks and rushing past the wheels of the 4×4. Taking the torch Elidi handed him, he turned it on, hoping to discover the vehicle was still drivable. He stood on tiptoe to look back the way they'd come, but could see no sign of anyone following. Still, he felt sure whoever was in the other car would have seen them.

He shone the torch on the wheel he'd felt break. It was worse than he'd hoped. The whole wheel had been pushed into the wheel arch, which had fallen onto the wheel, bursting the tyre and bending the wheel itself. Scott didn't know much about mechanics, but he knew that even if he could change the wheel, it would do little good – there was something more fundamentally wrong with the 4×4 than a flat tyre. He needed to think quickly and make a decision. They either waited it out for the night in the 4×4 and hope Mathew wouldn't see them, or they made a move now. Eve and her fear of heights meant there was a chance, the higher up they went, she would not follow them. He decided and turned to Elidi who was peering out of the window with Freddy beside her.

'We need to go. We'll take enough food and water for a few days. We can take the tent and find somewhere higher to camp.'

Elidi was obviously concerned but nodded all the same, and motioned for Freddy to put on his coat. Scott walked to the back of the vehicle and opened the boot. He took out a large rucksack that he'd packed with food and water. Taking two coats, he offered one to Elidi through the window and swung the other around himself, threading his arms through the sleeves. It took him a while to fasten the coat. He helped Freddy and Elidi out of the 4×4 and watched as they climbed a little way up the side of the brook to wait for him on the other side. He shrugged the rucksack onto his back and carried the small pop-up tent beneath his arm. After he climbed up to meet them, Elidi took the tent from him and strapped it to her back. Scott glanced at her swollen stomach.

'I'm sorry,' he said.

Elidi shook her head, reprimanding him for apologising. Again he heard their imagined conversation – how it wasn't his fault and he should not blame himself.

He shone the torch on the hillside ahead.

'We need to be careful,' he said, already breathing heavily. 'No slips, twisted or broken ankles.'

Elidi and Freddy watched on and nodded sombrely.

Scott took one look back at the 4x4, then turned and led the way up the mountain. As he took the first steps, he considered once again how everything had led to this moment. After all that had happened, it was difficult not to believe it was all determined, that he had no active choice in any of it. It was frustrating to see things that way, but it was impossible to ignore.

Already considerably higher than where the 4×4 had broken down, Scott scanned the horizon for any sign of Mathew and Eve. But all he saw was darkness. Maybe they'd gone straight past the turning he'd taken and were headed for Hassness House. If so, maybe it would be better if they found another vehicle instead of climbing higher up the mountain. If they could stay safe until daylight, then he would find another car – perhaps from the farm they had passed – and head south. He turned back to the mountain and led the way with more purpose, listening to Elidi and Freddy behind him, their footsteps heavy, their breathing laboured. He stopped for a moment and shone the torch on their faces. They were flushed, their expressions concerned and tired.

Then something made him turn off the torch. Movement to his left, down in the valley. It was a faint flicker, but he'd seen it: the sweeping arc of headlights.

FORTY-FOUR

EVE SHOOK her head as if waking from a deep sleep. She was breathing quickly, almost panting. Her skin crawled; she was fevered, damp, and alert to something she couldn't see or recognise. Her shoulders stiff, her legs exhausted, she stopped on her way up the mountain.

'Keep going,' Mathew said.

'Where are we?' she asked. 'What's happening?'

'Keep going,' he said again, turning back to the incline. 'You've got us this far. I need you to concentrate and tell me where Scott is.'

She remembered, vaguely, Scott's scent, leading her here. Then she recognised the feeling in her stomach, the way her scalp tightened and her throat closed up. Her fear of heights. She was unable to move her feet. Her legs loosened, folding beneath her.

'I can't,' she said. 'Where are we?'

Mathew ignored her. Shards of memories, sharp, came back to her. Gavin. She covered her mouth. It all came rushing back. What had she done? No – it hadn't been her. She saw it all as memories, but even now she was distant from them, apart from them. Gavin's body next to her, hands around his throat, squeezing.

'No,' she muttered. 'I can't have...' But it was all there, a record in her own head. But it hadn't been her! It was someone – something – else. She closed her eyes and held her head in her hands. What had she done?

'What have you done to me?' she shouted at Mathew. 'What's happening to me?'

Mathew stopped and turned, impatience in his expression.

'It won't last,' he said. 'Soon you will be who you were always meant to be. A New Human. This, now, is the old you fighting it. But it won't ... it can't last.'

'This is wrong. What I did ... it's wrong.'

'No,' Mathew said, 'it's not wrong. What you did was necessary.'

She couldn't go any further. Her fear of heights was just as in control of her as the AI was. She was helpless, and it angered her.

'You can't do this!' she shouted.

Mathew appeared unaffected by her anger, as though accustomed to it. He sighed, then relaxed his shoulders, waiting for Eve to disappear again; she saw it in his expression. And she felt it too. It wouldn't take long before the AI took control and she was lost again. Soon it would take over completely – she felt it.

She turned and began to walk down the mountain. She slipped, skidding on the wet ground, and fell. Getting to her feet, she moved more slowly, with more care, but again felt the earth beneath her shifting one way, then the other. Again she was on the ground. Something was stopping her – part of her that was out of her control. It made no sense and it was something she'd never experienced before. It made her nauseous. Disorientated, she crouched on all fours, her knees and hands wet and muddy.

'No!' she snarled.

Mathew, his hands on his hips, watched her, unmoved.

She was powerless.

'Give in to it,' he said. 'You will find peace when you finally give into it. Like the others.'

'I hate you!'

Mathew only nodded. 'All children feel that way about their parents at some point. It is only natural. But, like a good parent, I am not interested in your liking me. I want what is best for you – what is best for all humanity. You will help to change everything. You and the other four will herald a new world, one that is free from the depravity and coarseness of humanity.'

Rain fell harder.

'Now come with me,' Mathew said. 'This is the last thing you need to do before the AI completely transforms who you are. It is time Scott met his maker.'

'You can't do this,' she said. 'I won't do this.' But already she felt herself slipping away once again. The moments she was herself were ever more fleeting.

She stared up at the sky, still herself for now – whatever that meant. The stars – light years away. Behind them was time, gone for good, with no record apart from what she was looking at now. All of it had happened for so long with no acknowledgement from a creature like her. Billions of years gone by, with nobody to look back on it all and see it there, mapped out. Why was there something? Why was there not nothing? It would make more sense if there was nothing rather than something. But here she was, beneath the stars, beneath creation, and she felt it again, coursing through her in ones and zeros, in stuttering feeds of data: the Earth and its moon, the sun coalescing in swirls of matter until finally it was born with a silent flash in a dark corner of a galaxy, the purples and greens of nebulae, the rewinding of time into a smaller and smaller universe to a point where all light went out. She thought about plasma, about heat in a space without definition but everywhere and nowhere, and it rewound until she couldn't breathe and she couldn't think and it was there, like a black hole, pulsing, feeding, ready and waiting until the explosion, when it would vanish to the point at which everything started. And it was violet.

FORTY-FIVE

WHENEVER ANYONE DIED, Scott thought of the date tattooed on their hands. Even now, he considered that what happened was inevitable, unchangeable. Jean was an old woman, unlike the last two women they'd buried, who had been no older than fifty. George, being the only medically trained person in the group, did all he could to help, but illness and disease were no longer treatable in the way they had been before the Rapture.

Jean wanted to be buried. Scott thought this was a choice borne out of seeing so many people cremated. No one was buried any more.

They stood around the hole in the ground, in a cemetery in a village called Filindre, near Swansea. This was where Jean's mother and father were born, although Jean herself was born in Birmingham.

Four women lowered Jean's coffin into the ground. One of Jean's closest friends, Maddie, let out a loud sob. It was a reaction, but Scott and Eve turned to her. Scott looked away, but he noticed Eve staring. At fourteen, Eve had grown tall and gangly, her movements often awkward. He waited for her to make eye contact with him, so he could coax her away from staring. But she watched Maddie intently, her eyes narrowing and opening with each sob. Finally, he reached over and stroked Eve's back. She flinched at his touch, as if waking from a dream. She glanced at Scott then down into the ground, where dirt fell on top of the coffin from Gavin's shovel.

Scott recalled a funeral he had attended for a young man he knew when he'd been young. He'd been to several funerals, but this was the only one he'd been to when the person who had died was younger than he was. Scott was twenty-two. Women sang around the grave. The pain people felt was there on their faces, in the way they stood, looking as though at any moment they might collapse. It was because the man had been young and the way he'd died, in a car crash, was tragic. Dying young was different to dying old. It was an obvious thing to consider, yet it was still true.

Eve stared at the coffin in the ground.

She didn't understand, Scott thought. Or maybe she did. He'd lost count of the times he'd wanted to tell her, to explain it all. But he'd never done it.

He saw, in the corner of her eye, the violet colouring that appeared now and then. It was a sign, he'd thought, of her human and digital mechanisms coming together. The colour appeared to signal a confusion or conflict inside her. When she was younger, a tantrum, or even tears, often accompanied the change. It rarely happened but, when it did, it reminded him of what Mathew and Samuel had told him. He hated those moments. He recalled the word 'abomination', which Samuel had used that day. It was a horrible word, a vile description that had stayed with him.

A small bird flew into the row of hawthorn trees running around the cemetery, catching Eve's eye. She raised her head. Scott watched as she sighed then turned her attention to the people standing around the grave.

If what Mathew said was true, Eve was a New Human. And there could be others out there. Who knew how many children

Mathew had? Scott thought back to the women Freya had helped care for, locked away in that room. The sub-species of humans ran through his mind: Homo habilis, Homo erectus, Homo neanderthalensis ... There was a time when Homo sapiens lived alongside Neanderthal man. It was a strange thought – that two human species could co-exist, and even breed. But the evidence was there in the ground and in DNA. What species was Eve? He shook his head, attempting to rid his mind of the thought. But it was there again. She was a New Human, an ape that the AI had created – not through the slow process of natural selection, but through the selection of an intelligence humanity itself had created. The ultimate in artificial selection. She would not age, would not suffer illness or disease. When she had stopped ageing, she would know she was different. The AI, inside her, was mostly dormant, and it was only the violet in her eyes that was a physical sign of it. But the way she acted – often cold and detached – was most telling. He didn't want to admit it, and did a good job of ignoring it, but at some moments he was sharply reminded of how different she was.

He loved her. From the moment Dawn gave her up to him, he'd loved her and wanted to protect her. Whatever happened, he would be there. As he'd promised.

Funerals make you think of your own death. Maybe, he thought, Eve was thinking about this too. He looked across the grave at two boys standing next to their father. They couldn't be any older than nine or ten. Scott wondered why people weren't more envious of the young. But he wasn't envious – not really. It was an emotion he couldn't quite name, but he didn't want their youth; he wanted his own, as though his and theirs were not the same thing at all.

When the funeral was over, Scott and Eve returned to the house they'd adopted for the past two weeks. When he saw Eve later that day, he noticed she was reading a novel. He didn't want to disturb her, thinking, if he did, she might notice she was reading a novel instead of the non-fiction she devoured, but he wanted to get close enough to see what she was reading. Sitting near her, he waited to read the title of the book. She'd nearly finished. Tess of the D'Urbervilles. He caught his breath, remembering the first time he'd read the book and his emotional reaction to it. Eagerly, he waited to see how she felt when she finished it. As he waited, he tried to remember when she had last cried. He couldn't remember a time.

FORTY-SIX

WITH THE WEIGHT of Freddy on his back, Scott's thighs burned and his chest was on fire. Turning off his torch for a moment, he took a bottle of water from Freddy and drank it in one, hoping it would help. But the water stung his throat and chest and took what was left of the air in his lungs. He peered along the path towards the top of Scafell Pike, illuminated by moonlight. He glanced behind towards Seathwaite, knowing Mathew and Eve would be close behind. They'd seen his headlights and would have followed their tracks. He knew it. It would be easy for Eve to track him. He wanted to believe otherwise but deep down he knew it was hopeless.

'Are you going to be okay?' he asked Elidi, glancing at her stomach.

She nodded and gestured for Scott to continue along the path.

'I can get down,' Freddy said. 'I can do it myself.'
'In a while,' Scott said. 'A little further.'
The rain was at times welcome, and at others torturous,

turning the ground into a shifting mass that made it impossible to make headway at any speed.

He recalled Eve and the way her eyes changed. It was a gradual change at first, followed by an abrupt alteration in her actions and facial expressions. As she grew, now with hindsight, he saw how she was becoming more and more whatever the other thing inside her was. He picked up speed when he noticed a stone path a little way ahead and looked behind at Elidi, wanting to reassure her it would be easier going.

Scott continued for another five minutes before stopping and lowering Freddy to the ground. He sat on a rock and took water and, this time, food from Freddy's rucksack. His arms and legs shook with exhaustion. He handed Freddy a chunk of stale bread then chewed some himself, drinking water after each bite. A bird flew across the horizon, down in the valley they'd climbed from. The sky was moving towards morning. Elidi caught up with them and took several mouthfuls of water.

He set off again, pushing Freddy up higher on his back, and powered up the overgrown stone path that was on the verge of being reclaimed by the mountain. The rain had eased and the air smelled sweet and clean. The thought came to him that for any of it to mean anything required an animal like him to experience it. But that was a foolish thought, one that came from a sense of self-importance.

They were forced to scale a steep crag. Scott led the way, with Freddy below and Elidi last. The further he climbed up the crag, the more his mind raced: what would happen if his hand slipped and he fell to the rocks below? The thought made him stop and make the conscious decision not to fall – whatever it took.

The place he was heading for was less than an hour

away, hidden from the main path up the mountain. With heavy eyes, he peered behind and considered stopping again, maybe resting his head and eyes. Exhaustion was making him delirious.

A sound – a voice shouting? – made Scott stop and spin in a circle. He shook his head and listened, frozen to the spot. He closed his eyes, but all he heard was the rushing wind. Elidi had reached him again, a look of concern and then tiredness on her face. It was useless trying to explain what he was doing, because he knew it sounded crazy. He set off again with renewed strength, picking up Freddy. He didn't look further than the ground in front of his feet, not wanting the imposing landscape to demoralise him and slow him down. With each step his thigh and calf muscles fired and twinged, the small of his back throbbed, and his shoulders were tight and sore.

He walked automatically, his feet and legs no longer hurting. It might have been the last of his strength leaving him – a last gasp, emergency-fuelled impetus. There were people, in extreme circumstances, who had performed miraculous feats, like lifting a car or jumping several metres. Maybe that was what was happening to him. He stopped questioning it and let his body carry him the final few metres. He turned a corner – and there was the cave he'd remembered. It was different in the falling light and drizzle. Freddy breathed hard next to his ear and Elidi's footsteps rang out behind him.

He gasped, his legs almost giving way. He placed Freddy on the ground then fell to his knees. The rain fell more forcefully. Any of the remaining energy he'd found waned, and again he felt the urge to collapse right there on the ground and close his eyes. It would be easy to do – to rest his head and sleep.

'Scott!' Freddy said, holding on to his arm, trying to lift him. 'Come on! I want to do it myself.'

Scott nodded and got to his feet. Elidi was beside him too, helping him the last few metres. When he next lifted his head, he saw the cave up ahead.

'There,' he said. 'That's the place.'

Seeing it made the three of them speed up, their feet slipping on the wet ground, clambering up the last bit of shingle between them and the cave.

The moment Scott entered, the sound of rain vanished, to be replaced by the sound of three people breathing heavily.

'The tent,' Scott said, reaching inside the rucksack. He stumbled and fell.

Elidi was beside him. She motioned for him to stay on the ground and rest.

'I can put it up,' Freddy said.

Scott's body was on fire. He wouldn't have been able to help if he'd wanted to. In a daze, he watched Elidi and Freddy erect the tent. Moments later, they were helping him inside it.

With the three of them inside, Elidi looked at him questioningly. What now? What was his plan?

'We'll be safe here,' he said, and did everything he could to sound convincing.

FORTY-SEVEN

SCOTT STOOD inside the cave looking out and up at the moonlit sky, which was peppered with stars. He would never get used to the number of stars he could see, now there was no artificial light. Sometimes he was convinced he could see the turning of the Earth, or the galaxy, the stars stretching up and away in every direction.

Elidi and Freddy lay inside the tent, their eyes closed, either asleep or resting – he couldn't tell. If they could make it to morning it would mean Mathew had not followed them. Scott could make plans, look to find another vehicle and lose them again.

Eve had always been scared of heights. He hoped this would prevent her from following him up the mountain. But it was a long shot.

A gust of wind blew across the mouth of the cave. With it, Scott thought he could smell something different. It may well have been his imagination but, nonetheless, he returned to the cave and reached for his rucksack and the revolvers he'd brought with him. He went over his plan again in his head. If it was just Mathew and Eve, they had a chance. He checked both revolvers were loaded, pushed one into his coat pocket, the other in his rucksack, and walked out of the cave into the cool night. On one side of the cave was a sheer drop to a bank of scree that ran down the side of the mountain like a waterfall. He followed the edge of the drop towards the path they'd taken up the mountain. He peered down the track and into the valley. It was too dark to see, so he closed his eyes and listened. Only the wind. Then a wolf howling. Edging closer to the path down the mountain, he stretched his neck to see into the darkness. Shadows moving. Silhouettes. He took the revolver from his pocket and took slow footsteps backwards. He narrowed his eyes – he could be mistaken. More movement. Maybe a sheep, a wolf? He kept walking backwards. The sound of feet on hard ground, deep breathing, gasping...

'Stop!' He aimed his revolver at the dark figure. He couldn't make out who it was, Mathew or Eve. 'Stop!'

Eve's face dissolved out of the darkness and was now flooded in moonlight. He wanted to go to her but something was stopping him.

'Eve? Is that you?'

She stared back at him, her stare cold, her eyes violet.

'It's me. It's Sco—'

A hot, sharp pain shot through his leg before he heard the sound of a gunshot. He was thrown forwards. His gun went off, firing into the air, and he dropped it.

'Elidi!' he shouted.

'It's no use,' a voice said, a figure arriving from behind and looming over him. Mathew.

Scott tried to stand, but Mathew kicked him in the side, winding him. His hand and feet slipped on the ground.

'Eve?'

Mathew turned away and held out his hand. 'She's here. With me.'

He saw her eyes, more violet now than ever before. It was her fear of heights.

'Eve,' he said. 'What's happening?'

A look of confusion flashed across her face, and she shook her head.

'It's not Eve,' Scott snarled. 'I can see it's not her. What have you done to her?'

'It is her,' Mathew said. 'She is more herself now than she's ever been. It's only a matter of hours, maybe even minutes, until she becomes who she was always intended to be.'

Painfully, Scott tried to get to his knees.

'What is all this?' Mathew asked, pointing to the cave. 'You really make it difficult for me, don't you?'

'Leave Elidi and Freddy alone. I'll go with you.'

'It's not that simple anymore. I've waited all this time for the five New Humans to come of age. Do you really think I'd not have found you these past eighteen years if I'd wanted to? I let you have her. I let you bring her up. I wanted to see what happened to a New Human in a very human environment. And now I get to watch her kill you.'

'You can't do this.'

'I can't?' Mathew said. 'Really? Aren't you tired of going over the same old ground, time and again? I know I am. This is it – time to end it. Don't you think?'

Scott turned his attention to Eve. 'Eve, please. Don't do this.'

She peered back at him. It was no use. She wasn't the Eve he remembered.

Mathew walked past Scott towards the cave.

'No!' Scott said. 'Stop!'

Mathew ignored him, walking slowly but confidently to the cave. His feet made an ominous repetitive clicking on the stones.

'Eve?' He tried again. 'Don't do this.'

Eve tilted her head, stared straight through Scott, then followed Mathew.

The pain in his thigh was immense – molten hot. He got to his feet and followed Mathew and Eve, his leg trailing behind.

Mathew stopped. Elidi stood in the cave's mouth, Freddy holding on to her.

'Elidi!' Scott shouted. He stumbled and fell again.

Elidi walked out of the cave towards Mathew.

'Cat got your tongue?' Mathew asked, edging closer to Elidi.

Scott crawled to where he thought his revolver might be, but Eve was there before him, reaching for it. Without looking at him, she threw the revolver down the mountain. There was the faint sound of it colliding with the rocks below.

'He killed them all,' Scott said to her. 'Don't listen to him.'

Eve stared into his eyes but there was nothing there – no acknowledgement of the girl and young woman he knew. She turned away.

'I lied,' he said.

Eve stopped.

'I know I lied to you. But I wanted to protect you.'

Eve's head turned towards him, though she kept her back to him.

'That you were my daughter. A lie. That you were like everyone else. A lie. The tooth-fairy … all of it … lies.'

Eve took a step to one side, her slow moves threatening.

'But each lie was given for for what I thought was a good reason.'

Eve shook her head, her eyes darkening to brown before pulsing a deep violet.

'I'm not making excuses,' he said.

'Don't listen to him,' Mathew said, beckoning Eve over.

'I was wrong to lie to you,' Scott said. 'I should have told you the truth from the beginning.'

Eve continued towards Mathew and Elidi.

'Has Mathew told you what he did to your mother?'

Eve stopped again.

'Don't listen to him,' Mathew said. 'He'll lie to you.'

'Your mother didn't understand what he was doing to her. And he did the same to many other young women.'

Eve glanced at Mathew, who shook his head. 'He's lying,' he said. 'Your mother and I were in love.'

'Then what about the others?' Scott asked. 'The other four?'

Mathew stared at Eve. 'They're not mine. I'm not the father.'

'He is!' Scott said. 'He wants to kill off humanity – and leave behind his own children. You and the other four are his route to immortality.'

Mathew pointed his revolver at Elidi. 'Why can't you be like her and stop talking altogether? Really, Scott, it's becoming tiresome.'

'No!' Scott tried to run at Mathew, but pain shot through his leg from the bullet wound and he stumbled and fell.

Elidi, pushing Freddy behind her, walked slowly towards Mathew.

Mathew took a step backwards.

Scott held his breath. Elidi appeared both powerful and vulnerable, as if she knew some deep secret that was more profound than anything either he or Mathew could imagine. She changed direction and walked towards Eve.

Even Mathew waited to see what she would do.

Elidi stood in front of Eve. They stared into one another's eyes.

Scott gripped his leg.

Elidi's hand reached for her slowly, but Eve flinched. Elidi stopped, before trying again. Eve's violet eyes watched Elidi's hand. With the back of her fingers, Elidi brushed Eve's hair away from her face.

'Your eyes,' Elidi said. 'They're beautiful.'

Scott had forgotten the sound of her voice.

Eve's shoulders relaxed and she closed her eyes, leaning against Elidi's hand.

Mathew lifted his revolver then dropped it before looking back down the mountain. He backed away.

'Scott,' Elidi whispered to Eve. 'Whatever a father is, he was one to you.'

Eve's eyes were brown again. A look Scott recognised flashed across her face.

'Eve?' Scott said.

She sighed heavily. Her smile was sad and weak, but was there all the same.

'It's okay,' Scott said, getting to his feet. 'It'll be okay.'

'No,' Eve said. 'It's not. Nothing is okay any more.'

'Come back. Stay with us,' Scott said.

'I can't control it,' she said. 'I've done horrib—'

'It's not your fault. None of it's your fault,' Scott said. 'We will help you. We'll stop it.'

'You can't,' Mathew said, his revolver still on Scott. 'It's too late. Every time she has changed, it's lasted longer and longer. She will soon change and not change back. She is a New Human. She is the future.'

Scott shook his head and held on to Eve's arms. 'No. He's lying. We can help you.'

'You can't,' Eve said. 'It's happening. I can feel it.'

'It's over, Scott,' Mathew said.

Before Scott knew what was happening, Eve had pushed him aside and was spinning away.

Two gunshots, one fired by Eve and the other by Mathew, fired almost simultaneously, echoed around the mountain.

Mathew, clutching his chest, dropped his revolver and stumbled backwards.

Scott's attention moved from Eve, to Elidi, to Freddy. Each was staring at Mathew, who took another two steps backwards, then another, until finally his foot met thin air and he fell over the escarpment.

Eve fell heavily to the ground, clutching her stomach, where blood oozed out of a bullet wound.

FORTY-EIGHT

SCOTT SAT UP IN BED. He'd tried to ignore the voices coming through the wall, but the harder he tried, the louder the voices became. It had been his idea for Eve to spend more time with Becky, hoping she and Eve would become friends. It was the first time Eve had spent any length of time with a girl her own age. Becky was sixteen, Eve fifteen. Now, though, listening to Becky talking to Eve, he regretted the idea. He wanted Eve to stay the way she was and not be influenced by another teenager like Becky. But this was selfish.

'Gavin really likes you,' Becky said.

There was silence, and Scott imagined Eve's face screwed up in disgust. Scott shifted noisily on the bed, hoping they would hear him. He wanted to end their conversation, knowing how uncomfortable Eve would be feeling.

They'd found Becky a year earlier, alone, hiding from a Watcher. She'd survived on her own, in Sheffield, for nearly three months. Scott thought she might struggle to trust him and the others, find it difficult to integrate into the group, but she didn't. She became part of the group from the very beginning, and Scott recognised quickly that she might help Eve. Becky was full of life.

She'd smile and say hello to Scott whenever he saw her, and he'd hoped some of her vivacity might rub off on Eve.

Becky lowered her voice. 'Have you heard what people say about you?'

Scott sat up on the bed, tensed, ready to intervene.

'What?' Eve asked.

'That you're different.'

'Yes,' Eve said quickly.

'What do they mean?'

Eve sighed. 'I don't know.'

'Does it have something to do with your eyes?'

Again, silence.

'The colour,' Becky said. 'How they're ... sort of purple sometimes.'

'There are certain medical conditions,' Eve said, 'that can affect eye colour.'

'Is that what you have? A condition?'

'I don't know. Maybe.'

'Do you think you're different?' Becky asked.

'Yes. But isn't everyone?'

'Guess so,' Becky said. 'Shall I tell Gavin you're not interested? He really likes you.'

'I'm not interested,' Eve said. 'It's not as though he has a lot of females to choose from. There's you, me and Suraiya.'

'I'll tell him you don't like him. Even though he'll hate me for it.'

'I'm sorry.'

'Don't be. Like I said, it's your choice.'

Scott felt his shoulders relax.

There was the sound of movement next door.

'What are you drawing?' Eve asked.

'You,' Becky said, a smile in her voice.

'Can I see?'

'Sure. But it's not finished.'

'It's good,' Eve said after a short pause. 'You're good.'

'Thanks.'

Scott reached for his book and tried again to ignore them talking.

'I don't think you're different,' Becky said. 'Not in the way some of them are saying.'

'What are they saying about me?' Eve asked.

'That you're ... sort of cold. That you have no feelings.'

Scott held his breath, his chest tightening.

'No feelings?' Eve asked.

'Like I said, I don't believe any of it. You just keep yourself to yourself. There's nothing wrong with that. When your dad asked me to spend time with you, I wasn't sure th—'

'My dad asked you to spend time with me?'

Scott winced.

'It's not like that. He just said you spend a lot of time alone and that it'd be good to spend some time with other people.'

'You don't need to stay,' Eve said.

'It's not like that. I like you.'

'You're only here because my dad told you to spend time with me. Well, you don't have to stay. I'm fine being alone.'

'Yeah, but not all the time.'

Scott waited, scared to move.

'I'm sorry I said anything,' Becky said. 'I don't think your dad meant anyth—'

'It's okay,' Eve said. 'You should go.'

'I don't want to go.'

'Please,' Eve said. 'I want to be alone.'

'Your eyes,' Becky said. 'They're changing again. To purple. Sort of violet.'

Scott stood and walked to the door. A few seconds passed. He heard Eve's door open and close. He listened to someone – he *figured it was Becky – walk along the corridor and down the stairs.*

Scott walked to the window. It wasn't Becky, it was Eve. He took a step back from the window, scared she would see him. He watched her, in a thick coat, sit on the wall outside the houses on the opposite side of the street. She took a book from her bag and read. A fox with three cubs trotted along the street, the mother glancing at Eve and giving her a wide berth. Eve didn't look up from her book.

It was summer, but the evening was chilly. Scott dressed quickly, then went outside. 'Hey.'

She didn't acknowledge him. He sat beside her on the wall and the fox and her cubs darted off into a hedgerow at the far end of the street.

'I don't want you to ask anyone to spend time with me.'

'I shouldn't have,' *he said.* 'I just wanted to—'

'I know,' *she said.* 'But don't do that again.' *She lifted her head from her book.* 'Do you promise?'

'I promise.'

'Cross your heart?'

It had been a foolish thing to do. Scott cursed himself for upsetting Eve. Why hadn't he seen it as foolish before asking Becky? 'Cross my heart and hope to die.'

Her attention shifted back to her book. 'I'm okay on my own.'

She meant it. Scott saw it in her demeanour and heard it in her words. It wasn't self-pity or forced; it was genuine.

'I know,' *he said.* 'I won't do it again.'

'Thank you.'

Scott kissed her on the side of her head and walked back inside. He saw Elidi sitting in the dark kitchen at the far end of the hallway, beside the window.

'Elidi?' *he said.* 'Are you okay?'

She flinched and turned to face him. She'd been crying.

'Elidi?' he said again, moving closer. 'What's wrong?'

'It's Faisal,' she said. 'I know he's not coming back.'

Her husband had been gone for three days and had been due back yesterday.

Scott had thought the same as Elidi, but lied anyway. 'You don't know that. There's still time for him to come back. He'll be okay. George and I will look for him tomorrow.'

She turned away and looked out of the window, clearly unconvinced.

FORTY-NINE

SCOTT PRESSED his hand against Eve's stomach, applying pressure to stem the blood. He glanced over at Elidi, who was holding Freddy, checking he was okay.

'There's no time,' Eve said, panic in her voice. 'You have to help me. Mathew and the AI – I'm changing. For good. Into a monster. I've done terrible things.'

'He's gone,' Scott said. 'Mathew – he's gone. He can't hurt you any more.'

Eve shook her head. 'That doesn't matter. You must stop me.'

Scott pressed harder against the wound. 'What?'

'There's no time. You don't understand.' Panting, she pushed Scott away, then used both arms and hands to stand. She held her stomach, blood still spreading over her clothes and hands.

'We'll get help – find a surgical-machine.'

She was bent over, shaking her head. 'It's no good. It's happening.'

'What?' Scott asked. 'What's happening?'

'The AI – it's inside me. It's changing me. It's happening now.'

Scott took her arm to support her. She baulked at his touch and stumbled away from him, a flash of violet in her eyes.

'No!' Scott said. 'Fight it. You can stop it happening.'

Eve shook her head violently. 'I can't! I've tried. There is no fighting it.'

'What do we do?' Scott asked.

Eve's eyes were brown again. Doubled over, her hands covering the bullet wound, she lifted her head to Scott. 'You have to kill me. It's the only way. I can hear them in my head – the other four. It's happening. They're changing. Just like me. And there's no going back.'

'You're not making any sense.'

'It started when I left. I've been programming the AI and I got it to work again. Then I started to feel odd. Had blackouts – for days. I'd do things and not remember them afterwards. I started to have bad thoughts, dream about the other four like me. Mathew told me it's the AI inside me – it's changing me and I can't do anything about it.'

Eve cried out in pain. 'I killed him!' she said, tears rolling down her cheeks.

Scott peered over the edge of the precipice, confused. 'You had no choice.'

'No,' Eve said. 'Not Mathew.'

Scott frowned. 'Then who are you talking about?'

'Gavin,' Eve said. 'I killed him.'

Elidi gasped. Scott stared at Eve, shocked.

'I killed Gavin. I don't remember exactly what happened, but I remember parts of it, like it was a dream. I wasn't in control of what I was doing. It was as if I was a robot, doing what the AI wanted. When I did it, I didn't care – I had no feelings for him. It scares me.'

'It's a trick,' Scott said. 'It's Mathew. The AI. You didn't do it.'

Eve wiped the tears from her face and gave Scott a tired smile. 'I did. I killed him. Then I threw his body into the Thames. I did it.'

Elidi gripped Scott's arm.

'And I'll do it again. Unless you stop me.'

'I can't,' Scott said.

Eve's eyes flashed violet. She took her hand away from her stomach and stood up straight. Her body was healing, the nanotechnology inside her repairing muscle and tissue.

Eve strode towards Scott and Elidi, her eyes shining.

Scott raised his arms, trying to guard Elidi and Freddy. 'Stop!'

Eve stopped, shaking her head violently. She fell to her knees. 'You have to stop me! I can't fight it!'

'I can't do that!' Scott said.

'Please,' Eve said. 'I can't have your blood on my hands too. Please.'

Scott reached for Eve's revolver in the dirt. 'I can't!' he shouted.

Eve was on all fours, her head bowed. 'It's happening. They're in my head.' She looked at him, her expression with rage and despair. 'You can't stop them,' she said. 'They're not human. They look it. But they're not. And I'm not. You can't stop them.'

'There has to be another way.'

Eve crawled towards the edge of the escarpment and Scott followed, dragging his injured leg.

Eve raised her head. 'It has to be now.' She pointed to her head. 'It has to be here. It's the only way.'

Scott shook his head.

'I can't do it myself,' she said. 'It won't let me. So it has to be you. Before it's too late.'

Scott stared into her eyes. They were brown, and the girl he knew was still there. He and Juliet had taken her from Dawn and promised to look after her. The moment he saw her, he knew he'd do everything he could to keep her safe. And now he held a gun, ready to turn it on her.

'I promised your mother I'd keep you safe.'

Eve's shoulders fell. 'And you have. You've always been there for me. Even now, when I need you most.'

Scott bowed his head and stared at the revolver, held loosely in his hand.

'Tell me,' she said. 'Tell me the truth. Was it me? Did she die when I was born?'

Scott nodded slowly. 'Yes.'

'Sometimes it feels like I can remember everything. It's all stored away, waiting to be unearthed.' She pointed to her head.

Again, Scott focused on the revolver in his hand.

'Promise me you'll do it,' Eve said.

Scott lifted his head.

'Promise me,' she said. 'Cross your heart.'

It was too much. Time slowed. The stars, the moon, the spiralling arms of the Milky Way. And he was here, on the side of a mountain, a revolver in his hand, his daughter on her knees, waiting for him to end her life. He'd been there moments after her life began. Now he'd be there at the end too.

Eve's stomach had healed. She no longer held it, and the bleeding had stopped. 'Dad. Please. It's okay.'

Scott couldn't look at her.

'Cross your heart,' she said.

An emptiness spread through him.

She nodded.

Scott raised his revolver.

Her eyes were changing again. Her expression altered, her brow furrowing, pain etched across her face. 'Cross your heart,' she said seriously, with an edge of panic.

'Cross my heart,' Scott said and lifted the revolver again, pointing it at her head. He gasped for air, his heart thumping, his legs and arms shaking.

'And hope to die,' Eve said. 'Say it.'

'And...'

Eve's eyes turned violet and she stared through him.

Scott gripped the revolver and closed one eye. 'Hope to die!'

He fired. Eve fell backwards and over the edge of the mountain.

There was silence. All he could hear was the gentle pattering of raindrops against the wet ground. He dropped the revolver. Without thinking, he walked towards the edge.

'You don't have to,' Elidi said.

Scott ignored her. Carefully, he leaned over and looked down. Two figures lay at the bottom of the scree, motionless.

FIFTY

THE REST of the morning passed in a haze, the three of them in the tent for added warmth, a fire burning inside the cave. Scott had wanted to go to Eve straight away, but Elidi had convinced him to wait until sunrise. It was too dangerous in the dark and with the rain falling more and more heavily.

Scott closed his eyes and recalled the years gone by. He wanted to remember Eve as a child. He tried to count the memories he had of her and struggled to keep hold of each one as a truth; instead, his memories were vague and amorphous, impossible to pin down. He felt cheated. He wanted evidence that Eve had been there, alive, with him. The words she'd said, the people she'd known, the knowledge she'd collected. But now and then, he thought of her killing Gavin. How could she have done something like that? It hadn't been her. Each time the thought came to him, he had to work through it to the same conclusion.

Scott could only remember seeing the sunrise a handful of times. He watched the light change outside the cave, then inside the cave, until the forms of Elidi and Freddy took on detail and shades of colour other than the orange of the fire.

'Get your things together,' Scott said to Elidi.

Elidi, Freddy asleep in her arms, nodded. She'd returned, for the moment, to the woman she had been before.

Scott woke Freddy gently and motioned for him to follow Scott outside. Holding Freddy's hand, he walked out of the cave into the morning light. The rain had stopped, but the grey clouds threatened more. On the ground were jumbled footprints from the night before. In his mind's eye, he saw what had happened play out again. Next to the edge were Eve's footprints and the dents made by her knees.

The path down the side of the mountain was muddy and he took his time, constantly checking on Elidi and Freddy. As he descended, he kept the scree slope in sight as much as he could. The way down took them on a detour, but a manageable one. Finally they reached the bottom of the slope. They turned a corner and saw the loose rocks on which he'd find Eve's and Mathew's bodies.

'Wait here,' he said. 'I'll get her and bring her back here, then we'll take the main path down.'

He took off his rucksack, then stepped onto the loose rocks and scree. He imagined himself far above, looking down. What had happened the night before now seemed absurd, and he had almost convinced himself that the bodies wouldn't be there. But as he slipped on the loose stones, then regained his footing, he saw Eve's body, in the position he'd seen her last night. He waited, steeling himself for what he'd see when he got closer. He'd leave Mathew there. But he needed to take Eve with him. Somehow.

He scrambled across the loose rocks, looking for Mathew's body.

There was no sign of it.

The view from above might have been deceptive, he thought, and he continued to look. Making it to Eve, he went to lay a hand on her shoulder, but stopped. She was frozen, her eyes open and dark brown, the bullet wound stark in the centre of her forehead. Scott closed his eyes and covered his mouth. He turned away before opening his eyes. He stood and, filled with anger, scanned the side of the mountain for Mathew. He trudged across the loose stone, stumbling and falling, but there was no sign of him anywhere. Either he was looking in the wrong place, or somehow Mathew had survived and escaped.

Returning to Eve, he lifted her up and onto his shoulder. Even though she was light, he knew the distance and terrain he would have to cover would take its toll. But he couldn't leave her there, on the mountain.

Freddy was the first to see him. At first he looked excited, then he saw who Scott was carrying. Elidi held on to Freddy and made room for Scott to step onto the main path. Scott lowered Eve to the ground and took a seat on a rock.

'Mathew's not there,' he said, breathing heavily. 'Where the hell is his body?'

Elidi appeared confused. 'He has to be there. Maybe you were looking in the wrong place.'

'Maybe.' He looked up towards the cave. 'From up there, the bodies were close together.'

After a pause, Elidi said, 'He's dead. He's got to be. We saw him fall. And he fell all that way – he couldn't survive that.'

Scott nodded, but deep inside he wondered.

'I'll have to carry her down.'

'I'll help,' Freddy said unconvincingly, unable even to look at Eve's body.

'I know you would,' Scott said. 'But I can carry her if you carry my rucksack.'

Freddy nodded enthusiastically and strapped it to his back. It was huge on him, and Elidi helped adjust the straps.

'Can you carry her all that way?' Elidi asked.

Scott glanced at Eve and nodded.

He remembered Mathew stumbling backwards and disappearing over the escarpment. 'There's no way he could have survived that drop.'

'He can't have,' Elidi said, looking up at the sky. 'Before it rains again. It'll make the way down even more difficult.'

Scott lifted Eve onto his shoulders and started to walk down Scafell Pike.

FIFTY-ONE

IT TOOK the best part of the following day to get back to Hassness House.

Scott built the pyre using furniture from the house. Nothing had changed in eighteen years. He was still finding, then burning, bodies. It was all that was certain in life. The act itself was a performance, a routine or ritual he carried out, not thoughtlessly, but at least without conscious thought.

Elidi and Freddy stood outside the front door, watching him arrange Eve on the pyre beside the lake. They too were accustomed to what he was doing, but he felt that they were judging him and whether what he was doing was enough. He considered the construction of the pyre, its capability of generating enough heat, of lasting long enough, even the elegance of its construction, as though all of this should weigh the same as his affection for Eve. He'd taken his time building it, ensuring it would do the job.

He laid Eve on a door in the centre of the pyre.

When he was finished, he turned to Elidi, who nodded

and came to stand by him. She put an arm around Freddy and cradled her stomach with her other hand.

It was evening. Scott thought back to the night before, when they had made their way up the mountain. The sky was too dark now to distinguish the edges of the slow-moving clouds; it felt low and suffocating. He struck a match and lit a diesel-soaked sheet he'd pushed inside the base of the pyre. He circled the pyre and did the same in two other places, then stepped back and watched the flames gather in intensity, lapping the underside of the door. Elidi stood beside him, holding his hand. They moved further back. Freddy was at his other side, holding his arm. Scott felt his hand, still there, and imagined Freddy holding it.

The pyre illuminated the house and sky. Even now, after all this time, the fierceness of the flames, the intensity of their heat, amazed him. He always underestimated their ferocity and had to back away further, still with Elidi and Freddy holding on to him. The fire crackled and barked, shifting now and then until it had completely consumed Eve. At its centre, where Eve had been, the fire was an oval of white heat.

All that time and life – gone. Dawn's child – gone.

The fire always reached a point when Scott thought it would never stop, that it would consume everything. This was the moment, he'd learned, when the fire was at its most violent and primeval. It scared him, and he felt as though he was being let into a secret about the world. The fire roared, and he listened. Every fire he'd witnessed was the same one. Each was ancient. There was only one fire: whenever he called for its power to consume, it was there, ready and waiting. One day, he thought, man-made fire would go out and not return.

THE VIOLET DAWN

Elidi and Freddy went inside, leaving Scott to wait for the fire to die down. He watched the ash rise, spinning and jerking upwards and away towards the lake. The flames illuminated the path leading away from the house. It was on that path he had watched Dawn and her mother walk towards him. He realised that Eve was there too, inside Dawn. Dawn and Eve were both dead because he couldn't stop the inevitable. And that's what it always was – inevitable. It was exhausting, adhering to it all, following what had to happen. It was exhausting because it never felt inevitable – rather, it felt as though he was making choices for which he would have to take responsibility. Now, he was done with it all. He would stay in Hassness House, beside Lake Buttermere. Whatever came for him would come, and he would have to face it. But he would no longer run or hide, pretending he could change what would happen. Mathew, he knew, was still alive – somehow. It had to have something to do with the AI, with the healing properties Eve had. But Scott was finished thinking about Mathew and what he might do.

Scott watched the fire's final burst of anger before he went inside.

Freddy was in bed, asleep.

Elidi was waiting up for him, sitting in bed, candles flickering either side.

'It was a good pyre,' she said.

Scott sat on the bed and undressed. The orange of the fire illuminated the closed curtains.

'Where will we go now?' she asked.

Scott straightened his back. 'I'm tired of running.'

He didn't look at Elidi, but listened to her slow breathing.

'They will find us,' she said.

Scott's hand stopped and he sat motionless, his chest empty, the fight drained from him.

Elidi embraced him from behind, her arms holding him close.

He felt her swollen stomach against his back. 'He'll be here soon,' Scott said.

'He?'

'A girl would be too cruel,' he said.

Elidi pulled him backwards and into bed. He closed his eyes and was taken back to the building in Liverpool, where, upon the wall was written: *THE VIOLET DAWN IS RISING*. There were four others, who like Eve, were a new species of human. Elidi was right – they would come for them. Then he recalled what the AI said about having different plans to Mathew. What was it he said? A digital resurrection. It was all too much and again he felt his heart beating fast, a heat rising across his back.

'Shhh,' Elidi said. There were times he thought Elidi could read his mind.

He surrendered to Elidi's touch, but knew he would not sleep for some time.

FIFTY-TWO

SCOTT IMAGINED that the birth of a child would feel the opposite of death. But it didn't work out that way. During Elidi's day-long labour, all he thought about was death. He longed for Elidi's pain to be over. The birth of the child was secondary. The child was not there to account for its need to cause so much pain, so Scott sided with Elidi, who screamed and cried in pain. Freddy came and went, plucking up the courage to help, then retreating, only to return a short while later. Scott understood his dilemma and left the boy to manage it as best he could. Scott watched Elidi's face contort in ways he'd never seen before. She snarled and gnashed her teeth, crying, at other times raging. The changes he saw in her, he thought, were happening for good. There was no going back or changing what was happening – and Scott was a witness to it all.

Scott had found several books on childbirth and had read them. But none of that seemed to matter now it was actually happening. He had prepared well enough, with water and towels and even painkillers. But the real thing, the act of giving birth, was primal – the opposite of books and diagrams and instructions. Elidi did what she wanted to do, or what she needed to do. He was irrelevant. All the same, he watched and encouraged and tried to help.

When Elidi appeared to have no strength left, as though she had passed a test, the baby came. Elidi grimaced and cried, and then Scott had the baby in his hands.

It was a boy.

Her relief at hearing the baby cry made Elidi sob. Freddy was in the room when the baby arrived and he cried silently too – more in bewilderment, Scott thought, than joy.

Scott cut the cord and wrapped the baby in a blanket. It was bright red, all blood and heat, its eyes shut tight in anger, its lips pursed.

'It's a boy,' he said, placing him in Elidi's arms.

She smiled through her tears and cradled the baby.

At that moment, when he saw his son for the first time, everything changed again for Scott. Before that moment, he had been ready to give in to what would happen. But now the urge to run came over him. He wanted to collect everything that was precious to him and take Elidi, Freddy and the baby away, somewhere Mathew would never find them. He saw the future open up again. If they stayed where they were, Mathew would eventually come for them. No, Scott thought. They would run and hide. They would survive. He was not finished yet.

Elidi showed the baby to Freddy, who laughed with relief. 'Look at its bright red face,' he said.

Elidi touched Freddy's face. 'Say hello to your baby brother.'

'What's his name?'

Elidi glanced at Scott.

'River?' Scott asked her.

'River,' Elidi said to Freddy.

The birth of a child was time travel. Scott had been sent back to when every other child came into the world. The blood, the pain, and the wonder of it had been repeated time and again. This was what humanity was – it was an animal, breath and warmth. For a time at least.

Scott watched the three of them, together, and experienced a throb of pure happiness.

He turned to the window looking out onto the lake. The dawn light was changing from violet to pale blue.

No, he wasn't finished yet.

The end of Book Three

THANK YOU!

Thank you for being a reader and taking the time to read my book, the third in the Humanity Series.
I'm a new indie writer, trying my hand at writing sci-fi and dystopian fiction. For this reason, I am very much dependent on reviews. If you could spare the time, I'd be hugely grateful if you could write a review of *The Violet Dawn* for me.
And please visit sethrain.com if you'd like to stay in touch. I'd love to hear from you.
For now, all the best.
And remember: It's not the end of the world … only humanity!

Printed in Poland
by Amazon Fulfillment
Poland Sp. z o.o., Wrocław